RICK BUSH

INVERTED PUBLISHING

Front cover artwork by Monica Laita

For my parents, who can now tell people I do something respectable.

LEAGUE OF FRANKENSTEIN

CHAPTER ONE

THE PORTAL

Lightning raced across the night sky, illuminating Peter and Wendy as they raced up the intermittently dark driveway towards Frankenstein manor. The rain fell heavily, covering the pair with fat droplets.

Wendy rang the doorbell and Peter looked up to the heavens to witness lightning spit from the clouds and hit the rooftop above them with another huge crash of thunder. Wendy screamed and held onto Peter tightly as sparks fell around them. Peter tried the door and found it open.

'Come on,' he said and swept his hand over his messy hair. 'He's expecting us.' Peter pushed open the door and he and Wendy rushed inside.

The hallway, which led to the laboratory, always seemed a little unnerving. Their footsteps echoed off the tiled flooring and left wet marks where they trod. Jars of pickled animals and body parts lined the shelves, all looking down on them while they made their way towards the large wooden door, where they could hear Victor's machines powering up.

In the lab, they saw the machine that the Doctor had been working on. No longer a multitude of pieces but finally formed into what looked like a giant camera lens, poking out of a shiny cylinder. It aimed towards the far wall and Victor had hooked it up to the electrodes connected to his giant batteries, which the storm powered.

The noise from the machinery was almost deafening. Sparks flew from the unseen cables that littered the ceiling. Wendy and Peter stopped in the doorway, hesitant to go in.

'Doctor Frankenstein,' Wendy said. 'Is it safe?'

Victor turned to see his two assistants and lifted his goggles onto his head. A clear sign of excitement showed on his face. He was in his late twenties or early thirties. Wendy had never exactly found out how old he was. Surely at least ten years older than her and Peter's sixteen years.

'Quite safe, my dear Wendy, just stay back!' He looked over at Peter, who stood marvelling at the equipment brought to life. 'Peter, I'm glad you're here.'

'Does this mean you've done it?' Peter said.

'We'll soon see.' He walked to the switch on the wall next to his enormous batteries, dodging some errant sparks. 'As soon as we have enough power from the storm, this device should open a portal to Neverland. One more lightning strike should do it.'

Victor looked wild with anticipation. It had taken a full year to adapt his reanimation machine into the device that stood before him. If this machine could open a doorway to that incredible dimension with such wondrous beings that never grew older, maybe, just maybe, that was the key to bringing his wife, Elizabeth back to life.

Wendy turned to Peter and saw the hope in his eyes. She knew exactly who he was thinking of.

'It's been so long,' she said. 'Do you think she'll still be there?'

'I don't know if she even cares anymore,' Peter said. 'Four years - and she never came looking for me.'

'I still don't believe you were once able to fly, Peter,' Victor said.

Peter smiled to himself. 'The magic wore off years ago. Besides ... I'm all out of fairy dust. I don't know how I'll be able to thank you, Victor. I've dreamed of seeing Neverland once more.'

'No thanks are necessary.' Victor looked over at Elizabeth, who floated in her bubbling cryogenic tank, which had preserved her in suspended animation for years now. The long scar on her chest, a cold reminder of his failure over a year ago. 'Science hasn't helped bring my wife back. Maybe what I need is a bit of magic.'

Lightning flashed through the windows of the laboratory, lighting up every corner. Outside, a gargantuan lightning bolt hit the antenna on the roof, and Victor's lab once again burst into a frenzy of activity.

'This is it,' Victor said. He grasped the lever on the wall. 'Shield your eyes!'

Wendy and Peter both covered their faces, but peeked over the tops of their hands. Victor lowered his goggles and pulled the lever.

The device powered up and sent a beam of bright blue energy from its lens into the far wall of the laboratory. The three of them watched in astonishment as a bright blue grid projected onto the wall, disappearing into a horizon of impossibility, surrounded by fluorescent pink lightning.

The fabric of reality itself stretched and pulled apart around the edges of the portal, and vapour poured out from inside the neon spectacle that danced before them. Once clear, they could see the grid forming a tunnel and, at the end of the tunnel, a cloud formed, and behind it an entire moonlit vista came into view.

An island became visible, with exotic pirate ships floating in the night sky, and an ocean of such intense blue surrounding it, reflecting the lunar light. An enormous fire burned in the forest on one side of the island, lighting up the nearby trees.

'Neverland!' Wendy cried, pulling her hands away from her face. 'That's Neverland.'

'Home,' Peter said, and a smile beamed across his face. He grabbed Wendy's hand.

Victor looked uncontrollably excited. A look of such accomplishment grew on his face.

The portal shook and sparked violently. Victor looked over at his switches and dials and saw them all pointing to the red.

'Too much power ... it's unstable ... hold on!' Victor flicked switches, channelling the power output through more filters, but the dials didn't come down. Now the entire room shook and the portal glowed bright white. Victor ran to the lever and turned it off, but before the energy subsided, a bright flash engulfed the room. The portal, with its glowing grid-like structure inside, disappeared. A figure landed on the ground with a thump. Vapour rose from its shoulders. And, just above the figure, a bright purple light darted around.

'My God.' Victor raised his goggles and stared at the two beings before him.

As the smoke cleared from the room, the figure stood up from her crouched position. A woman—a pirate no less. Her long red hair flowed over her shoulders, and the dirty purple bandana she wore matched her purple gloves and boots. Her waist-length black naval jacket clung to her tanned skin, and numerous belts hung from her waist like flat, leathery snakes, and turned into a slithering skirt.

A small, purple fairy hovered above her left shoulder, and darted around, seemingly confused. Her bright plasma-like wings were a purple blur of motion behind her with sparkles of purple dust falling from them. Her short black hair swooped down over one eye, slightly covering the eye-patch held in place over it. She seemed to be wearing some kind of dark armour around her shoulders, wrists, and calves, which glowed with bright purple lights. She didn't wear much else apart from short black underwear, which showed off her trim legs, and black and purple chest armour that left her stomach exposed.

The pirate looked at the three strangers in front of her and her eyes focused on Peter. He looked back at her and down at her missing left hand—a shiny metallic hook took its place, and seemed to glow with energy.

'Hook?' Peter asked.

As if in answer, the pirate woman raised her left arm and held her hook up to her face.

'Like father ... like daughter ... Pan,' Hook said with scorn, and her false metallic hand transformed, moving into her arm until her entire wrist opened up and an energy cannon emerged. She aimed her arm at Peter and fired, sending a bolt of bright purple plasma towards him. Peter leapt onto the floor and the bolt hit Victor's equipment behind him.

Hook fired more energy bolts at Wendy, who Victor shoved out of the way. Morgan flew across the room and laid punches into Peter, who tried to stand.

'Stay down,' Victor said to Wendy, and dodged another blast, running from behind the giant stone slab in the centre of his lab towards a cabinet full of his inventions. He collided with the cabinet, and a metal gauntlet landed on him. It was something he'd been playing around with—an electrically powered glove that could send a pulse of electricity through the palm. He planned one day to sell it as a medical tool, to jumpstart someone's heart.

The tiny, aggressive fairy punched Peter in the face, and he staggered back at the might of her minuscule fist. He swung his arm toward her and slapped her across the lab. Hook watched as her tiny partner in crime flew past her, hit the wall, and fell to the floor in a puddle of purple fairy dust.

Victor used the distraction to lunge at Hook. He grabbed her breast, then cranked up the juice on the power glove. Hook screamed and convulsed with shock, and then backhanded Victor across the face with her cannon hand, sending him flying across the room.

With a savage look in her eye, Hook spied Wendy scuttling across the floor towards Peter. She grabbed her by the throat and lifted her clean off the ground.

'Wendy!' Peter yelled.

'Ahh,' Hook said, and looked at her captive's

terrified face. 'I've heard so much about you.'

'Get off her,' Peter said as he darted across the lab towards Hook with his fists clenched. Hook dropped Wendy to the ground and snapped her hand around Peter's throat when he collided with her.

'Not quite the boy you were, are you, Pan?' she said and threw him into Victor's wife's cryogenic tank.

Hook took a moment to look around. 'We're on Earth. I've heard such nice things.' A smile grew upon Hook's face as though a plan formed in her mind.

Wendy scrambled away from the pirate. Victor gritted his teeth and lunged for the portal device.

'Wendy,' he yelled. 'The lever.'

Wendy got to her feet and grabbed hold of the solid wooden handle and pulled. Sparks flew all over the lab. Victor twisted the portal device so it aimed at Hook.

The fairy, flew up to join her.

A beam of energy fired from the device's lens and engulfed them both. The glowing blue grid opened up around them, and pink electrical energy flew out and grabbed their bodies. Victor gritted his teeth while he fought to hold it in place. All of a sudden, it pulled the two intruders into the grid and sent them hurtling towards its horizon.

In a bright blue blast of light the grid faded and the portal closed. Wendy released the lever and the lab grew quiet once more. She looked over at Peter, who got to his feet, holding his bruised neck, and looked over at Victor.

'Did you send them back?' she asked.

'No,' he said. 'Not enough power. Maybe moved them ten miles away, but at least they don't know where to find us.' Victor fixed his eyes on Peter.

'I thought you said it was a paradise?'

'Apart from the pirates.' Peter shrugged.

Wendy was shocked at how violent Hook's daughter was. She'd never even heard of Hook having children. Neverland had always seemed like a place of fun and adventure, but perhaps she remembered it wrong? She'd always recalled it as playing, but had she actually been fighting? Had Peter, in fact, been leading an army of children to their potential deaths?

Wendy took Peter by the hand. 'What do we do?'

'I have to stop her,' Peter said.

Victor walked past them and headed to something he'd seen at the far wall.

'But how?' Wendy said. 'You don't have your powers anymore.'

Victor picked up a pinch of purple fairy dust and held it up in his fingers. 'Maybe all you need is a bit of magic?'

RICK BUSH

CHAPTER TWO

NEVERLAND

Tootles picked himself up off the forest ground and wiped the blood from his mouth. He looked over his shoulder. Hook's giant hovering pirate ship followed him. He got to his feet and ran when the searchlight from the ship lit up his position.

Three pirates descended from the ship on ropes and landed on the forest ground, not far behind Tootles, and gave chase.

The savage grown ups caught up with the young ten-year-old and lifted him into the air. Although he kicked and screamed with all his might, he made no match for the three vicious pirates. The largest of the three, Bill Jukes, threw him against a tree with a blood-curdling crunch of bone. When Tootle's broken body hit the forest floor, Jukes pulled out a pistol and aimed it at the boy's head.

'Wait,' Hook said as she floated down from her ship. Morgan hovered down with her and whispered into her ear. Hook landed gently on the ground and walked up to the lost boy.

'What do you mean, wait?' Jukes asked. 'We should kill each of them on sight.'

'If you have any brains at all, Jukes, you'll listen to me. Now stand down.'

The towering, muscular pirate lowered his gun, and Hook's frowning face turned to a smile when she fixed her eyes on the child.

'Now then, little boy ... where are your merry band of brothers? Hmm?' She leant over with an evil grin on her face.

Tootles lifted his bruised, swollen arm and pointed into the sky behind her. 'Right there.'

Hook turned around to see another of her giant floating pirate ships headed straight for hers. On the deck, instead of her loyal pirates, stood a group of children with Tinker Bell hovering at the helm.

They piloted the ship straight into hers and, with an almighty explosion, the side caved in and a bevvy of splinters fell to the ground, as did the entire ship, but now in two pieces.

The boys cheered as their ship lowered to the

ground and landed next to Hook. She loved that ship. The three pirates with her backed off, as she had rather a short temper.

She looked over at Tinker Bell, who still stood on the vessel, and raised her left hooked-hand. Slowly, it transformed into its cannon form and she fired a blast from it.

Tinker Bell and the lost boys leapt from the ship as the energy bolt hit. The little fairy flew over to Hook, who turned to her purple hued fairy partner.

'Morgan,' Hook said. 'You told me you'd take care of that annoying insect.' The evil fairy took off and headed straight for Tinker Bell, with her vibrating purple wings shining brighter and brighter, engulfing her in a giant purple light, from which she emerged the size of a human suddenly.

Tinker Bell enveloped herself in a bright green light, grew full size, and collided with Morgan. They spun around, throwing punches at each other, and grappled as they flew their way through the treetops.

'How can you do this?' Tinker Bell said. 'Giving her all that power has destroyed our home.'

'I am glad of it, sister,' Morgan said in her raspy, whispering voice. 'You shunned me anyway. Serves the lot of you right for being so mean.'

The dark sprite punched Tinker Bell in the face, and they both landed on the ground, skidding along the leafy floor until coming to an abrupt end at a thick tree stump. Morgan stood. Her sister lay unconscious at the foot of the tree. She raised her hand and it glowed purple with energy. Finally, she would end the bitter rivalry. With one blast, Tinker Bell would be no more.

Morgan's partnership with Hook had started when the now-deceased-Captain's daughter rose to power among the pirates. Carefully, she took over each ship and conquered each Captain that had emerged in James Hook's absence.

The pirates loved her.

They loved her viciousness, her ability to get what she wanted, and that hair; that luscious, long, curly red hair could hypnotise anyone. At last, she had an entire armada at her beck and call, but while she'd been building her devoted army, Tinker Bell had been busy recruiting Lost Boys. They would arrive on the island, confused and upset, but that glowing fairy would take them to Pan's old hideout.

Morgan would watch Tinker Bell play her games with the boys and the Indians and, though she constantly tried to join in, Tinker Bell wouldn't allow it. It was her gang, she would say. Go find your own. So she did. She sought out Hook and made a deal—a partnership—and showed her the secret powers of the mystical fairies of Neverland.

After all, the humans who had come to be stuck in Neverland stole all their technology from the fairies. The naïve, young humans called it magic, of course, and the fairies were all but glad to keep some of their secrets hidden. Better that they were seen as a mystery, as these humans seemed hell bent on destroying each other. But this Dark Sprite had come to see the influence of humans on her sister and all of Neverland. It was no longer their realm, and she plotted to rid her entire world of these stupid beings. So, she struck a bargain with Hook and gained all the powers she'd ever wanted. Wondrous magical powers that Hook could not comprehend but was more than happy to use to start a war with The Lost Boys. Something for which she'd been longing for a long time. All Morgan had to do was sit back and watch the humans destroy each other until none remained.

To find herself standing over her sister, about to kill her kin, was not what she had planned, but this was war. A war she'd started.

Morgan stared down at Tink with hate in her eyes and watched her sister moan in pain. Try as she might, she could not bring herself to do it. Her fight was with the humans, the boys, the pirates, and the Indians.

'Please, Morgan,' Tinker Bell said and opened her eyes. 'Don't do this. I know I pushed you away ... I know that. And I'm truly sorry, but you must stop this war. People are dying. Can't you see that? You have unleashed something terrible upon this world.'

Morgan lowered her arm and powered down her fist. 'Maybe the world deserves it,' she said.

Tootles ran out of the trees and stopped suddenly when he saw the two fairies. Morgan saw him and glanced back at Tinker Bell with a sly half-grin creeping over her face.

'No, 'Tinker Bell said. 'Don't do it.'

Morgan raised her hand and, though Tootles tried to run, the energy blast hit him square in the face, frying his brain and evaporating the blood oozing from his nose.

He fell to the ground with a thud. Morgan activated her wings and flew off, leaving Tinker Bell screaming for murder.

Tinker Bell activated her bright green wings and flew back through the trees, back towards her Lost Boys, but she already knew the fate that awaited her. The sounds of swords penetrating young flesh and the gargled screams of innocence lost echoed through the forest as Tinker Bell watched Hook slice up her friends with her hooked metal hand. The deadly pirate unclipped a sword's hilt from her belt, activated a glowing purple beam of energy, and cut through body after body, leaving a sizzling mess of limbs and torsos surrounding her. Her bloodthirsty smile made even the most hardened of pirates question their actions, but they would never dare to say that to Hook.

Hook deactivated her power sword and clipped it back on her belt. Tink headed towards her at speed.

With a flick of her long red hair, Hook flew up into the sky, and Tinker Bell darted after her. They soared past the treeline and up into the sea of stars.

Hook looked back and saw the little fairy gaining on her. She transformed her hook into the cannon and sent blasts back towards Tinker Bell, which she only just managed to block with her energy powers. Still, the impact hit her hard, and she plummeted into the ocean.

Tinker Bell's head burst out of the waters and looked up at the red haired menace.

Morgan flew up to Hook and looked down at Tink. The two of them looked down at the carnage they had caused. The fire from the crashed pirate ship still burned away in the forest on the side of the island.

Suddenly, a terrific explosion rocked the sky behind the two and threw them into the clouds.

Tinker Bell managed to hover out of the water and flew up to see the source of the blast. She witnessed the night sky fold in on itself and rip open to reveal a glowing, blue grid structure disappearing into the distance with pink lightning striking it. After a few seconds, an image formed at the far end of the grid: A room with three people staring through the hole in space.

'What is this sorcery?' Hook said.

Morgan looked on intently. 'I'm not sure.'

Then the bright neon hole in the sky pulsed and the pink electricity poured through it, reaching out to Hook and Morgan, grasping them and pulling them towards the bright gateway.

The two villains were sucked into the portal. Tinker Bell flew up to the strange hole in space. When she saw who stood on the other side of the glowing doorway, it took her aback.

A little older but unmistakeable.

'Peter?' she asked herself. Hook and Morgan disappeared into the bright blue grid, which flashed once more and then was gone as if being deleted from existence. Tinker Bell was left floating in the night sky, alone.

CHAPTER THREE

AN AWFULLY BIG ADVENTURE

With care, Peter reached under the bed of his small bedroom in Wendy's family home. Neither of them could remember the last time he had got it out, let alone tried it on. Wendy watched while Peter stretched underneath the frame and found something. He slid out a raggedy old suitcase and hesitated at the latch.

Peter took a breath and opened the case, revealing his old Neverland clothes. They appeared old and leathery green and black. The vest looked worn and scratches covered it. Battle scars from his adventures. His green leather wrist braces brought back memories; he could remember Tinker Bell helping him put them together. The leather-covered special magical armour, she had told him. And, now, the brown fingerless gloves looked a lot smaller than his hands.

Underneath the costume lay the brown belts and straps he used to cover himself. One belt held the holster for his power sword; the magical weapon that had been a gift from Tinker Bell and her people for saving Neverland from Captain Hook. He had missed holding its powerful shaft in his hand and feeling the power hum through it.

'Will it even fit you anymore?' Wendy asked.

Peter held up the tight black bottoms, highlighted with green leather down the sides.

'There's only one way to find out,' he said.

Wendy laid out the costume on the bed. Peter undressed. He felt nervous. After all, it was Victor's device that brought that wicked pirate here. It shouldn't be up to Peter to clean up his mess. But Peter felt he had a responsibility and, secretly, he'd been longing for an awfully big adventure.

As Wendy helped Peter on with the otherworldly clothes, he felt just how tight they fit. He would wear belts wrapped around his legs back when they were twelve, as if he'd strapped the costume to his body, but now they seemed to fit like a second skin. The vest fit snug but Peter was still rather skinny, and his bare arms remained free to move. The wrist braces and gloves still fit but his boots, however, did not.

'I don't think you're going to get into these,' Wendy

said, holding up the small boots. 'Here, use these.'

She picked up the large brown boots he'd use in the winter, and Peter pulled them on, covering them with the scratched, brown shin guards that strapped around each leg, covering up to his knees.

Wendy handed him his power sword, and Peter stood, holstering it in his belt. He looked awkward. Wendy held up a small pouch that Victor had filled with the evil fairy's purple fairy dust.

'Do you remember how this works?'

Peter took a pinch of the glowing dust. 'To be honest, I feel more nervous than happy right now.' He sprinkled the sparkling energy particles over his head and body and Wendy stood back.

Peter closed his eyes and clenched his fists. The fairy dust did something to him. He'd never thought that much about it before, but it felt like drinking alcohol. His mind tingled, and he felt looser and more energetic, and oh how he had missed it. But, try as he might, his feet would not leave the floor.

'I don't feel anything,' Peter said, frustrated. Wendy took his face in her hands and moved her lips close to his.

'You will,' she said and kissed him deeply.

A surge of endorphins rushed from his brain and through his body. Now it wasn't just his mind that tingled—every part of him seemed to be awash with energy. Peter kissed Wendy back. It took a while before either of them noticed that they had floated up six inches from the bedroom floor.

———

High above the rooftops of London city, Hook and Morgan hid among the clouds, and lightning danced around them in the distance, lighting up their faces.

'What kind of bargain do you mean?' Hook said. 'You promised me the power to take over Neverland, and now you're saying we're stuck here? Wasn't it your sister who would happily make her way here with Peter Pan all those years ago? How do we get back?'

Morgan flew up to her ear and spoke in her whispering tone, 'I just think this is an opportunity you shouldn't miss. The journey from Neverland to this place is a long-kept secret I never learnt from Tinker Bell, but it seems the scientist we saw has created a device that can open a doorway between our worlds.'

'So we find him and use his device to get back?' Hook asked, wondering just what her little partner was hinting at.

Morgan now hovered around Hook'sother ear. 'The device that brought us here could also transport an entire armada of ships.'

'Now I see,' Hook said. 'I conquer this world, leaving you with Neverland. Is that it?'

'Remember who gave you this power. The kind of

devastation you could cause would give them no choice but to surrender to you. You would be invincible. An entire planet at your feet, rather than a mere island.'

'Very well, little one,' Hook said. 'You help me get my ships here, and I'll let you have your Neverland.'

Hook smiled, hungry with the thought of battle with these civilised fools. Even Peter had become older and useless. Morgan fluttered down, looking over the city.

'Show them you are unbeatable,' she said. 'And they won't even put up a fight.'

Hook descended from the sky, her cannon hand glowing with energy as she stopped in the air fifty feet above Tower Bridge. She blasted a bolt of energy from her arm and watched as it effortlessly sailed through the air and hit the concrete, sending multiple vehicles flying, exploding into flames. The screams started, and soon the finger pointing, as they became aware of her presence. Hook made sure the people below could see her while she fired blast after blast towards them, sending the scared little people running. But they couldn't run fast enough. The bricks and mortar from the southern tower exploded at its base, and the entire bridge collapsed on top of motorists and pedestrians alike.

Hook flew across the skyline, causing random destruction, and showing just how dangerous she was. She revelled in the screams and the sound of crying— this was where she was meant to rule. These people would see her as a God.

'Such a pathetic world,' she said to herself. 'Is there no one who can even challenge me?' As if in answer, a figure swooped across the sky and came to a halt, fifty meters from her. Peter held his fists on his hips and gave a sly smile.

'I'll challenge you,' Peter said. The wind had blown his hair around, and his locks seemed to have a life of their own as if gravity had no effect on them. Hook looked back and relished the thought of defeating her father's killer. Maybe he wasn't as old and useless as she'd thought.

'Pan,' Hook said. 'Found your wings, did you?'

'I defeated your father. I'll defeat you too.' Peter grasped hold of his power sword and held it up, lighting the glowing energy beam, which formed a blade of pulsating green light.

Hook took hold of her power sword and ignited it, lighting her beautiful, evil face with a glowing purple hue. They flew toward each other and clashed swords.

———

Peter could see she was a gifted swordsman, but he had been doing it for much longer than she'd been around. In fact, he wasn't quite sure just how long he'd been alive, since he'd never aged in Neverland.

Hook's attacks felt ferocious, but Peter stood his ground, blocking and parrying each strike. Hook managed to shove Peter a good ten meters away with an almighty swipe of her blade, clashing against his, sending him tumbling backwards down towards the ground. He managed to right himself just above the burning streets below, and Hook made her way down to him.

Her sword skills seemed excellent, but Peter wondered how used to flying she was. Maybe if he took her for a ride around the city, he'd be able to gain the upper hand.

He put away his sword and flew above the streets, with Hook in pursuit. Peter made his way across the Docklands and over the river Thames, where he soared through the burning remains of Tower Bridge. He looked back to see Hook fly through the flames, firing her cannon hand at him. Peter dodged the blasts. He should take their fight away from other people.

Once more, he flew up into the sky and gained some distance from Hook. Then he turned and ignited his sword again. Hook propelled herself towards him and fired a bolt of energy. It rocketed towards Peter, and he swung his sword with all his might, hitting the energy blast, and sent it hurtling back towards Hook, hitting her square in the chest.

She fell from the sky, tumbling helplessly until she crashed onto the top of the burning remains of part of Tower Bridge. Her sword hilt fell out of her hand. Peter flew out of the sky and landed elegantly a few feet away, in front of several burning vehicles.

'These powers must be new to you,' he said with a grin. Hook reached out her hand, and her sword propelled through the air and into her clenched fist, where she ignited it.

Peter raised his sword again and lit the blade. The two fighters ran at each other like two jousting knights, past flaming vehicles and strewn crumpled bodies underneath fallen masonry. They clashed and skidded along the rubble as they turned to face each other. Another clash of energy blades and Hook's cannon hand glowed. She shot out a beam of electricity, which Peter blocked with his blade, but the force of the strike brought him down to one knee. The power increased as Hook got closer, but Peter managed to swipe his blade at her arm, sending the electricity beam flying over his shoulder and hitting a double-decker bus behind him, which exploded into flames.

Peter brought his sword down with some force, but Hook blocked it. Locked in a struggle, each of them tried to force the energy blades closer to the other's face.

Peter felt in his element. This wasn't just a fight to save London; this was fun. He smiled at Hook and winked. She raised her left hand and the cannon transformed into its hook formation.

Hook seemed in no mood for games. This was to be war and a serious one at that.

She swung her arm and hit Peter across the face with

the sharp blade of her metal appendage. Peter cried out in pain and held his face. Blood fell from between his fingers, and half his cheek hung from his face.

'Over there, Doctor Frankenstein,' Wendy said, looking out of the window of Victor's car at the explosion on the decimated bridge.

'My God ... the destruction,' Victor said and put his foot down hard on the accelerator. The car pulled up onto Tower Bridge and screeched to a halt, bringing the smell of melted rubber from the tyres.

Victor and Wendy ran from their vehicle just as the police arrived, and though the uniformed men tried to stop them from heading onto the burning bridge, Wendy shoved them out of the way and ran towards Peter with Victor right behind her.

She screamed out, 'Peter!'

Hook kicked Peter in the chest and sent him falling backwards. He dropped his power sword. Hook turned hers off and ambled towards the bleeding hero. Peter tried to get to his feet but could only manage to get to his knees. He looked up at Hook, still holding his face together. Her arm transformed back into a cannon. She glanced at Wendy, who ran towards them, and turned back to Peter.

'My father sends his regards,' Hook said and blasted

a hole clean through Peter's stomach.

He fell to the ground—just another casualty among the many on Tower Bridge—as Hook, looking pleased with herself, flew up to the night sky to re-join with Morgan.

'No,' Wendy yelled and dropped to the ground beside Peter, where she put her arm around his body, lifted his head, and cradled it in her arms. Tears streamed from her face and dripped onto his chest. Victor crouched down and took Peter's carotid pulse.

'I'm so sorry, Wendy,' he said in a solemn voice.

'There must be something you can do, Doctor Frankenstein ... send her back.' Desperation broke her voice. If only Victor could just press a button to send Hook back, but this situation would require more than either of them could give right then.

Victor rested a hand on her shoulder. 'I think we're going to need some help.'

CHAPTER FOUR

VAN HELSING

Alice pulled at the rope that tied her hands to the back of the chair. It wouldn't budge. This vampire, Lord Ruthven, obviously knew his knots. Maybe if she could break the back of the chair? The pale, skinny vampire approached his other hostage—a young man who worked for the London Underground. Alice and her employer, Barbara Van Helsing, had tracked the monster from central London into the deep railway tunnels that lay beneath the city. In the squalid, dank maintenance room, the smell of old blood haunted her nostrils, and she cursed herself for getting separated from Van Helsing. Her mentor had her taught better than that; Van Helsing had given her a purpose in life and she didn't want to betray that trust.

—

It had been six months since Alice ran away from the asylum; at least she thought she'd run away. She didn't have any actual recollection of planning an escape or even escaping, but one day they were strapping her down and shocking her head and the next she found herself outside the asylum, seemingly free but wearing a strange blue outfit, covered in electrodes and wires.

Alice kept to herself for the next few weeks, sleeping rough on the streets of Oxford and living off the kindness of others, but only after creatures of the night attacked her did true sanctuary come.

The vampires had been stalking the homeless for weeks, and even Alice had heard about it from the newspapers but hadn't believed them. Even she, who felt certain she'd visited a wondrous world filled with incredible talking animals and vicious playing cards, couldn't quite believe that such fantastical evil creatures could truly exist.

Her proof came in the form of a gang of monstrous street urchins—boys no more than fourteen, maybe, and only a couple of years younger than her. They surrounded her in an alleyway, but just as the gang stalked Alice, Barbara Van Helsing had been hunting them.

She seemed to appear out of the shadows, just as the vampires did, and her moves were swift and aggressive. With beautifully fluid movements, Van Helsing drove two stakes, which she'd strapped to her chest, into the hearts of two of the creatures. They screamed and burnt up into dust before Alice's eyes. Before long, Van Helsing dealt with the others equally, and Alice's saviour stood before her.

Van Helsing wore a long brown coat and a black hat, which matched her dark clothes. Though her appearance gave her entrance a dramatic flare, Alice first noticed the woman's eyes. Such burning bright blue as if bursting with vitality, and her bright blonde hair hung in stark contrast to her surroundings. She looked like a giant, standing so tall, and almost towering over Alice.

The expression on Van Helsing's face—one of intense confusion and fascination—said that it wasn't Van Helsing who was so giant, but Alice who had shrunk down to the size of a peanut.

Her blue uniform seemed to have strange abilities, and as soon as Alice grew back to normal size, Van Helsing took her in. Shortly after that, she trained Alice in the ways of vampire hunting.

Alice had often wondered what had happened in that asylum and how she'd escaped, but even when she thought she remembered a glimpse of it, her memories got twisted with her strange Wonderland fantasies. She was crazy, and she knew it. She felt sure her parents thought it too. Why else would they send her there? Alice never did try and contact them. Besides, she was having too much fun hunting Vampires with Van Helsing.

Lord Ruthven grabbed the poor maintenance worker's face and squished it in his hand. He pushed his head back and walked over to Alice, who still struggled with her bonds, trying to ease her foot out of the rope around the legs. If only she had been able to get that damn shrinking costume to work again, she'd be able to get herself out of situations like this.

She looked over at the bag of weapons she carried for Van Helsing, which lay on the ground at the far end of the room—so close but so totally out of reach. She wondered if Van Helsing would come at all. Lord Ruthven circled behind her.

'She will come for you, yes?' he said, smiling his toothy grin.

'Oh, she'll come,' Alice said in her cockney accent. 'And when she does, you and your master won't know what 'it you.' Alice hoped to get some insight into this mysterious Master they had heard several vampires speak of.

Lord Ruthven's grin dropped from his face.

'What do you know of the Master?' he asked.

Slowly, Alice looked up at him and smirked. 'I know you're his slave.'

Ruthven struck Alice across the face with the back of his hand, sending a trickle of blood down her plump bottom lip.

'You foul wench, you know nothing.' Ruthven almost spat the words out at the top of his voice. 'He is undying ... all knowing ... he will feed on this world and make it his own ... and neither you nor your whore mistress can do anything to stop him.' Lord Ruthven spun his head towards the door and sniffed the air.

A smile grew on his face. 'Van Helsing.'

'Now you're in trouble,' Alice said. 'She kills things like you for a living. She knows every fighting style there is. She's studied black magic and can choke you with a single thought.'

Lord Ruthven held the worker's neck and pierced his flesh with a sharp fingernail. Blood oozed out. The vampire smiled.

'You will all die, and the Master will reign free,' he said.

'No,' Alice said. 'Don't kill 'im.'

'You like him, do you?'

'I swore I'd protect 'im,' Alice said. 'And though I may have delusional psychosomatic fantasies ... I'm not a liar.'

With great aplomb, Ruthven said, 'Then you have already failed. The Master looks down upon the two of you from his high castle ... and laughs.'

'So your Master lives in a castle?' Alice asked.

Ruthven frowned. 'What?'

'That's all I needed to know.' Alice pulled her right foot free of its bonds.

Ruthven took out a knife and darted at her. Alice yanked her entire body backwards as hard as she could, rocking the chair over and kicking Ruthven in the face as she toppled over onto her back and broke the chair into pieces.

Lord Ruthven fell to the ground near the maintenance worker's feet. Alice scrambled to the bag of weapons and strapped it to her back.

Lord Ruthven got to his feet. 'You're crazy.'

'So they say,' Alice said, and then pulled out a giant croquet mallet—the one weapon she insisted always lived in the bag.

She felt ready for action; if she had to take on Ruthven all by herself, then so be it. The vampire gave an almighty roar that truly unnerved Alice, his eyes lit up with intense anger, and he lifted from the ground.

Van Helsing burst through the door, already pulling an arrow from her quiver. This one had a glass bulb on the end, filled with white powder. She fired, smashing the bulb on Ruthven's chest and releasing garlic particles into the air around him. He choked and fell to the ground. Van Helsing threw the bow away. Her Dutch accent sounded thick when she yelled, 'Alice, the sword.'

Alice wasted no time and pulled the samurai sword from her bag, and then threw it to Van Helsing, who caught it just as Ruthven ran towards her.

Van Helsing swiped at the vampire, but Ruthven leapt over her, clung to the corner of the ceiling, and brandished his teeth with a hiss. Van Helsing threw the sword at him, but the vampire slapped it away and darted across the room, then landed on Alice. When she fell, her weapons spilled from her bag and covered the floor.

She grabbed her mallet and held it at Ruthven's throat, stopping him from biting her. Van Helsing pulled a stake from the belt strapped across her chest.

'Send it back this way,' she shouted.

Alice looked at the wild creature on top of her, brought her knee up into its groin, and slammed the croquet mallet into its side as hard as she could.

This manoeuvre forced Ruthven towards Van Helsing, who threw him over her shoulder, smashed him into the ground, and plunged the stake into his chest. An enormous fireball rose from his body, and a cloud of ash settled in its place.

'Not bad,' a voice from outside said.

Van Helsing raised the stake, ready for whoever came next.

Victor Frankenstein walked into the room and surveyed the carnage and the look of relief on the man tied to the chair.

Van Helsing lowered the stake.

'Victor Frankenstein,' she said with a smile. 'How did you find me?'

'It's difficult to miss you these days,' Victor said. 'Word of your vampire hunting sells many a newspaper.'

Alice untied the maintenance worker, who seemed sweaty and disoriented.

'Victor, this is my assistant, Alice,' Van Helsing said while getting to her feet, and then turned to Alice. 'She's a little crazy in the head, but she knows how to use a croquet mallet.'

Alice tried to ignore that remark and, instead, focussed on what sounded like a compliment of her fighting skills.

Victor raised his eyebrows. 'A new assistant? How many is it you've got through now?'

'What's he mean by that?' Alice asked, pulling at the ropes tying the man's hands.

'Ignore him, my dear,' Van Helsing said. Her smile turned to discontent. 'Why are you here? Still pining after your dead wife? Still looking for a way to bring her back from the dead?'

Victor was visibly angry. 'You speak like it's not an admirable thing I'm trying to achieve.'

'The dead should stay dead.' Van Helsing, raised her stake once more. 'I should know that better than anyone.'

Victor stepped forward. Alice watched him closely. He'd come here with a purpose.

'London is under attack,' he said. 'And I need your help.'

'So you missed me,' Van Helsing said with a sarcastic tone. 'Why else would you come here? I hunt monsters ... I am not a soldier.' Van Helsing turned away from Victor and walked towards Alice and the man, now untied and being helped to his feet.

'This invader uses magic from another world,' Victor said. 'She is far more powerful than any soldier. But a team can be greater than the sum of its members.'

Van Helsing glanced over at him. 'I don't work well in a team. If you'll excuse me?'

Doctor Frankenstein walked out of the room. Van Helsing stood there, looking at the dark tunnels beyond the door, and Alice approached her.

'So that was Frankenstein,' she said. 'You always described 'im as being older and crazy.'

'Put him out of your mind,' Van Helsing said.

'He's talking about what happened to Tower Bridge, isn't he?' Alice said. 'The flying woman.'

Van Helsing raised her voice, 'It's not our concern.'

While they continued to argue, the man behind them hunched over and went into spasm. The sounds of his dying body went unnoticed. He held his face in his hands, quivering. With a deep breath, he finally dropped them, transformed, and gave an almighty roar as his canine teeth grew into sharp points.

'Bloody 'ell, he was bitten,' Alice said. Quickly, she slid across the floor, grabbed the samurai sword, and threw it to Van Helsing, who swung the blade at the creature and sent its head flying off. The head landed on the ground with a thump, still alive, still gnashing its teeth, and looking around. Its body kept walking towards Van Helsing. She thrust the sword through its chest, impaling its heart and pushing it out of its body, through its back.

'Wood,' Van Helsing yelled. 'It has to be wood.' Alice grabbed a pencil from the desk behind her. The body grabbed Van Helsing's hair and pulled the woman towards him.

Alice plunged the pencil into the exposed heart, and the body let go. Van Helsing kicked him away, and he burst into flames, as did his severed head—screaming silently, as much as a head with no lungs could scream.

'So much for saving 'im,' Alice said with a sigh.

The two vampire hunters walked back through the tunnels towards the exit.

'What good do we do if we just end up killing everyone?' she asked.

Van Helsing tried to deflect her question, 'We were just too late.'

'And what about Frankenstein? If London really is in trouble, do we just stand and watch 'til it's too late?'

CHAPTER FIVE

LORD JOHN ROXTON

Watkins had tried explaining to the Brigadier just how complicated it was to track down the location of the ancient ruins, but the old man just couldn't comprehend what would take so long. He had agreed to fund the project on the understanding that valuable treasure would be discovered with ease, and now he found himself in deepest Africa trying to keep himself as cool as he possibly could in a makeshift tent with the worst coffee he'd ever tasted in his life.

Lord John Roxton and Enid Challenger had been gone since the early morning and supposed to be back already with a detailed map of the surrounding area. The Brigadier couldn't stay much longer in this place—

not with only Watkins and whoever was manning the radio—Perkins was it? Hopkins? Too many Kins to remember.

'Well blast, man, how long does it take to find a bloody necklace?' the Brigadier asked. Watkins walked over and handed the old man a mug of coffee-flavoured boiled water.

'Oh, it's more than just a necklace, Brigadier,' Watkins said. 'The Amulet of Cthulhu was thought to be mystical. It had the ability to sap all magical powers from whoever wore it. A binding spell, if you will.'

The old man looked at Watkins as if he'd just asked him to smell his underwear.

'Magical powers? Who writes this nonsense? Is it worth anything? That's what I want to know.'

'But, Sir, it's for the museum.'

'If it's pretty. If it's worth any spondoolies, it goes in my pocket.' The Brigadier took a sip of coffee and tried his best not to scrunch up his face in disgust.

'Excuse me, Sir?' a voice at the opening of the tent asked.

'What is it, Hopkins?' the Brigadier said.

'It's Thompson, Sir.'

'Yes, yes ... what is it, man?'

'Urgent telegram for Lord John Roxton.'

The Brigadier sighed; Roxton had come begging for him to help fund his excursion to deepest Africa. And how could he refuse? Roxton had received a lot of attention and publicity last year when he discovered dinosaurs still living on that mysterious island in the South Pacific, so—naturally—the Brigadier had jumped at the chance to be involved in another discovery like that. But a necklace? What kind of fame and glory would that bring? Nothing, if he didn't get back soon. Just where the hell was he?

———

Roxton pushed his way through the thick jungle vines, chopping them apart with his large machete. A tall man, he boasted broad shoulders, which held a sturdy head full of brown hair. His chiselled features hid behind a couple of day's growth of facial hair, and sweat dripped from his brow. Strapped over his worn shirt, a pair of black Colt 1911s nested into holsters, which hung under his armpits.

He pulled off his fedora and his circular sunglasses and ran his fingers through his hair. Then he put his hat back on and pocketed his sunglasses. With a tight grasp on the machete, he made his way forward, breaking through to the sheer cliff edge that he and Enid Challenger had found that morning.

Below, lay the ancient temple of Cthulhu, half-buried under the ground, half-destroyed but magnificent nonetheless. He had promised Enid an adventure ever since meeting her at her father's house in London.

Professor Challenger had shown proof to the world that dinosaurs still existed, and Roxton had helped him get that proof. He and Enid had hit it off immediately, and Roxton felt eager to head back to that lost world to bring back live samples of some of the seemingly extinct species that lived there. For certain, that place held more secrets. However, the Professor absolutely forbade his daughter from going—far too dangerous—he said. And though Roxton knew how to handle himself, he also knew not to get on the wrong side of Professor Challenger. So Roxton had put his focus elsewhere for the time being and organised an expedition to locate this ancient temple and retrieve the mythical Amulet of Cthulhu.

Roxton climbed down the rope, back to where Enid waited in the temple. He'd mapped out the surrounding area and felt positive he could now lead the rest of the expedition party back to the ruins where they could all decide what to do with the Amulet.

A few hours earlier, when Enid and Roxton first walked into the Temple, a giant stone statue of the terrifying Cthulhu himself met them. A huge godlike creature with the head of an octopus, complete with tentacles cascading down from its face, on top of a body of an anthropoid dragon and giant folded wings on its back.

The Amulet lay hidden in a worship room, which they accessed via a small door at the foot of the statue.

The inscriptions on the wall showed great detail and told how, if the Amulet were to be taken from the temple, then the great protector would bring death to all its thieves.

Roxton insisted this was superstitious nonsense, but Enid insisted that they should bring the others to decide what to do.

Roxton stopped descending when he heard voices. German voices. And then he saw the German trucks parked by the side of the temple. How had he not noticed them sooner? Too eager to return to Enid, he supposed.

The German soldiers marched Enid out of the temple, towards their officer. Roxton grasped the rope tightly as he watched the officer shout and then slap Enid.

Roxton reached down and grasped his gun. More soldiers came out of the temple, this time carrying an assortment of jewels, treasure, and the box containing the Amulet. One of the soldiers shouted, trying to get the Amulet back inside the temple. Obviously, he'd seen the inscription for himself.

'Damn Nazis,' Roxton said to himself. He'd heard that Hitler had his army seek out all sorts of mystical trinkets from all over the world, much like himself, but he'd never expected to see them here, in Africa.

The soldiers showed the bounty to the officer, who waved them over to the trucks. The officer then pulled out his Luger and forced Enid into the truck furthest away.

A surge of adrenaline pumped through Roxton's body as he slid down the rope with one hand and fired his gun with the other.

He landed on the ground and, by running through the trees, dodged a barrage of machine gun fire from the Nazis. Roxton reloaded his gun and poked his head out from behind a trunk. The men now sat in the three trucks and drove away.

Roxton ran as fast as he could, fired at the driver of the last truck, and hit him in the back. The soldier in the passenger seat raised his machine gun and fired at Roxton, sending dirt flying into the air around his boots. Roxton leapt for cover, rolled along the floor, took half a second to aim both his guns, and put four bullets into the soldier's chest.

He watched the two remaining trucks. The second one contained the Amulet and the first contained the officer and Enid, who he could hear screaming for him. They disappeared into the thick jungle behind the temple.

Roxton grabbed a large stone brick from the rubble at the foot of the temple and ran to the stopped truck. He placed the brick on the passenger seat and pulled the soldiers out before setting off after the other soldiers.

Soon, Roxton caught up with the other trucks. He pushed the brick into place on the accelerator and climbed out onto the bonnet. He sped up behind the larger truck with two soldiers in the front cab and two in the rear, still steering with one hand behind him. They saw him and grabbed their guns.

Roxton leapt from the bonnet into the back of the truck, knocking the soldiers down as the truck he'd abandoned, veered off and crashed into the trees behind them. He grabbed one of them—the one he'd seen arguing about the precious necklace—and shoved him hard against the back of the cab.

'The Amulet,' he yelled. 'Where is it?'

Behind him, the other soldier picked up his gun and raised it at the two of them. Roxton grabbed his guns, pulled them out of their holsters, and spun around. He emptied half of each of his magazines into the soldier, propelling him out of the back of the truck where he hit the ground in a splash of blood.

The solider pointed to the box beside them.

'Take it,' he said in his thick German accent, looking panicked. 'But we cannot escape the protector. I saw it ... in my dreams.'

Roxton punched the soldier in the face, which knocked him out. Then he holstered his guns, grabbed the box, and took out the Amulet. The gem inside glinted a reddish-green colour that he couldn't quite place or put a name to.

Quickly, he pocketed the necklace. Just then, the two trucks skidded to a halt. Roxton pulled himself up onto the roof of the cab as the two soldiers got out and aimed their guns at him.

Roxton somersaulted forward off the roof when they fired at him, pulled his guns out, and shot back while he spun through the air. When he landed on the ground, rolling along the jungle floor, the two soldiers already lay dead. He aimed his weapons at the Nazi officer, who held Enid at gunpoint.

Roxton hoped the Officer hadn't been counting the bullets he'd fired because Roxton had. He had one bullet left in each gun, and he had to make them count.

'Put ze guns down, Mr Shooty,' the officer said, pushing his Luger against Enid's head.

'All right,' Roxton said. 'Just … don't hurt her.' He lowered the scuffed and worn guns and placed them on the ground gently.

'Now hand over ze Amulet.'

Roxton pulled the necklace from his pocket and held it up. The three of them watched as the gem vibrated and glowed.

'What are you doing?' the officer asked.

'I can assure you it's not me,' Roxton said.

'The inscription,' Enid said.

The entire ground beneath them shook, and they all looked back toward the temple.

From over the top of the treeline, Roxton saw the fifty-foot-tall statue of Cthulhu stomp its way toward them. Debris fell from its joints with each thundering step it took. The monolith stretched its arms wide and came for the Amulet.

'Du hurensohn!' the Officer swore and raised his gun at the oncoming giant and fired.

Enid pushed her hands against her ears and ducked out of the way.

'Over here, quick,' Roxton yelled, and Enid ran toward him and into his arms. The officer kept firing as the giant statue of Cthulhu stood over him and looked down. The bullets bounced off its rock-like skin, and the statue lifted its enormous foot. Roxton and Enid ran as the giant brought its foot down on the Nazi Officer with an almighty crunch of flesh and bone. With a satisfied look, the statue turned its attention to Roxton, who still held the Amulet.

'Get in the truck,' he yelled. 'Go.'

Enid climbed into the truck with Roxton. The statue made its way over to them. Its epic steps caused tremors.

'No keys,' Enid said.

Roxton looked over at the squished mess that used to be a Nazi officer and screamed at Enid to get out of the truck again.

They ran between the creature's legs just as it stomped down on the truck, causing it to explode. Roxton and Enid hit the ground. The statue raised its leg from the burning wreckage of the vehicle. The explosion had destroyed the outer layer of the foot and exposed a metal framework inside. The giant rock creature looked to be some kind of robot. It stood down on its mangled foot, but the ankle section gave way, and the entire edifice fell to the ground. It smashed through trees and vines and shook the ground. A huge cloud of dust filled the area. When it cleared, Roxton saw that the statue had sustained damage; its midsection had a hole in its rocky outer skin. Underneath lay a collection of pistons and pneumatic systems.

'Head for the trees,' Roxton said, and as Enid ran for cover, he ran for the only remaining truck. After pulling the petrol cap open, he tore off a part of his shirt and pushed it inside, leaving a small section poking out. The statue tried to get back up. Roxton lit the end of the piece of clothing, then raced to the front of the truck and got in the driver's seat. The truck started straight away, and Roxton already felt that this was a bad idea as he slammed his foot on the accelerator and darted towards the fallen statue.

The rocky giant pushed one hand against the ground and lifted himself up slightly. No way could Roxton get the truck into the hole while the statue was off the ground, so he pulled the steering wheel to the right and aimed for its leg, which still lay against the ground. The truck hit it, and Roxton drove up the leg of the statue as the creature continued to pull itself up.

Roxton shoved the gear stick into neutral and dove out of the door. The truck hit the hole dead on and exploded inside the giant's stomach, sending metal piping and wiring everywhere. The statue exploded into two, and both pieces crashed down to the forest floor with another enormous ground-shattering thump, which sent another cloud of dust and fire up into the air.

Enid stepped out of the tree line. Horror made an O of her mouth and widened her eyes. Frantic, she looked around for Lord Roxton.

'John?' she shouted. 'Please ... John ...'

Roxton strolled out of the dust cloud with soot all over his face and tatters of shirt hanging from his ripped body. He stood and held up the Amulet, smiling.

'Piece of piss,' he said in his well-spoken voice and slid his circular sunglasses onto his nose.

By the time Roxton and Enid returned to base camp, the Brigadier had grown furious.

'Where the bloody hell have you been?' he said. 'I'm not funding this little escapade just so the two of you can dilly dally about and rip each other's clothes off.'

The punch, although not that forceful, was unexpected and took the Brigadier by surprise, knocking him unconscious and onto the ground. Enid shook her fist in pain and shrugged at Roxton, who pulled out the Amulet and waved it above the slowly-waking officer.

'Don't worry, I've got a lovely piece of compensation here,' he said. 'Selling it to the museum won't exactly make us rich, but the story attached to getting it may make us famous. And isn't that what life's all about?'

The Brigadier just murmured and tried reaching out

to grab the Amulet, but missed it. He grabbed a few more times, evidently dazed and seeing triple or even quadruple.

Watkins walked over, holding the message they had received earlier. 'Urgent message from London, Lord Roxton.'

'Just Roxton,' he said. 'I may sound like a Lord, but I don't act like one. Who's the message from?'

'Victor Frankenstein, Sir.'

'Charter a plane home, Watkins.' Roxton glanced over the message, and excitement lit his eyes.

Enid put a hand on his shoulder. 'What is it, John?'

Roxton looked out into the distance, seeing all the possibilities of what it could be. Frankenstein was crazy but a genius, and if he needed Roxton's help it would mean a lot of coverage in the media.

'Riches and fame,' he said to her. 'Riches and fame.'

CHAPTER SIX

ASSEMBLED

Hook walked toward Buckingham Palace, and the onlookers gawped at her insolence. The British Army had been called out and had collected at the gates to the palace as soon as Hook made her plans known.

She'd told the entire country she would be taking up residency there as the new monarch, and should the people of Britain prefer there to be no more bloodshed, they should all walk away and let her stroll in.

As she headed toward the large gates at the front of the palace, the military had still not had their instructions. Were they to fight? Take her on and surely die? Or should they pull back and let her walk in?

As if in answer, the police moved the civilians out of

harm's way, two tanks pulled into view outside the gates, and aimed their cannons at Hook and the tiny fairy hovering next to her.

The tanks fired. Hook held out her hand, putting up a force field, which shattered the projectiles. With a smile, Hook took on the entire assembled military might at the gates until no one would oppose her.

Amidst the wreck of burning metal and bodies, she strolled into Buckingham Palace—her new home.

———

Victor showed Alice her room and helped her with her bag of clothes. Alice looked around; her eyes wide and shining.

'This whole room's mine?' she asked.

Victor smiled and lifted her bag onto the bed.

'Well, I didn't plan on anyone else sleeping in here.'

Alice walked over to the bag and opened it. When she set about unpacking, Victor walked to the door.

'I think Barbara is downstairs. When you're ready, come down, and I'll make some tea.' About to leave the room, he stopped when Alice lifted out a pair of blue overalls with electrodes running through the seams. 'Where did you get those?' he asked.

'This?' Alice asked. 'This is what I was wearin' when I escaped from the asylum. I think it's special ... I mean ... it does things ... it made me shrink to the size of a penny.'

'Can you show me?' Victor asked.

Alice shook her head.

'I can't get it to work again; must be out of power.'

Victor held the costume and took a closer look at the electronics.

'You say you were wearing this inside the asylum?'

'Well, I don't remember puttin' it on. I just woke up wearin' it. I had strange dreams at the hospital, but the doctors knew what they were doing. They'd give me pills to 'elp me sleep. And they must've worked 'cause I ain't had a single one of those crazy dreams since.'

Victor could see this girl had been through hell. Just what had the doctors in that asylum done to her?

'Well, maybe I could take a look at it?' Victor said. 'I tell you what, if you come to my laboratory, we could see if we can get it working again.'

Victor led the young girl through his maze of a house, into the laboratory on the ground floor. After taking a few minutes to look at the strange uniform and finding no power source located on it at all, Victor asked Alice if he could run some tests on her.

'I'm not all that fond of being poked and prodded again, to be honest, Doc,' she said.

Victor assured her that nothing he would do would be invasive. If she managed to shrink while wearing this device, then he wanted to find out how she managed it.

Another twenty minutes had elapsed before Van

Helsing walked in, looking for them. The sight of Alice with electronic devices all over her brought a flush of anger to her face.

'Victor,' she shouted. 'What are you doing? Alice, are you all right?'

'Yeah, I'm fine,' Alice said.

Victor jotted down some readings and looked up at Van Helsing with a smile. 'It's incredible. Why didn't you tell me about this suit before?'

'We just got here,' Van Helsing said. 'You've managed to get that thing working? She still looks full-sized to me.'

'No, it's not the suit that makes Alice shrink.' Victor ran over to his blackboard and wiped off some old diagrams for artificial limbs. Once there, he drew an atom with a proton at the centre and circled by an electron. 'Look, this is your basic everyday atom. Proton in the middle. Electron whizzing around it. But the rest is simple, empty space. If you were able to reduce or compress the space between the proton and the electron, the atom would effectively be smaller. Of course, the electromagnetic force keeps the distance from ever reducing.'

Victor rubbed out the atom diagram and drew a human body. 'But Alice is different. Her body's electromagnetic field can fluctuate. It's probably what caused her bad dreams and possibly her ending up in that hospital.'

'So I'm not crazy?' Alice asked.

'I didn't say that. Fluctuations in your body's electromagnetic field are absolutely going to mess with your brain. I think the doctors at that hospital saw this and started experimenting. It looks like they built this suit to amplify your EM field fluctuations, altering the very nature of your atoms, reducing the energy of the electromagnetic barrier between the protons and electrons of each and every atom in your body, and allowing you to miniaturize.'

Van Helsing crossed her arms. 'That sounds completely crazy.'

'And a doorway to another dimension, filled with flying pirates is completely sane,' Victor said. 'I think they managed to get it to work by inducing a state of unconsciousness and letting Alice roam around in a delusional state, believing she was dreaming of shrinking and growing larger, when in actual fact she was doing just that.'

'Can we get it to work again?' Alice asked.

'With a bit of tinkering around, I think I can get it to work without having to put you to sleep, yes.'

'Alice, come and eat something,' Van Helsing said. She then showed an excited Alice out of the lab. Van Helsing looked back at Victor and made sure he looked her in the eye. 'Please, be careful, Victor. She's young. Don't break her.'

Van Helsing stood at the window of Victor Frankenstein's living room and looked out onto the streets of Greater London while the sun disappeared into a horizon of smog. Alice took another bite of her cake and turned the page of the newspaper.

'Van Helsing ... how does he expect us to fight this woman?' she asked. 'She's only been living in bloody Buckingham Palace for six days now.'

Van Helsing had been thinking the same; so far Hook had been content living the good life, ordering enormous feasts of food and demanding the country's wealth of riches be brought to her. But soon, surely, there would be more destruction. Orders and rules for the everyman. Her rules. Capital punishment for thought crimes. It was too much power for one person to have; she wouldn't stop with Britain. The World would be next unless Frankenstein could figure out a way to stop her.

Victor walked in with a guest. 'Barbara, Alice,' he said. 'May I introduce Lord John Roxton. The greatest big game hunter there's ever been.'

Roxton eyed Van Helsing.

She looked back at him as he approached her; he seemed like the kind of man who thought the world owed him everything. A macho adventurer who spent his family fortune on gallivanting around the world, looking for fame.

'The legendary Barbara Van Helsing. You are truly a beautiful creature.' Roxton took her hand and kissed it.

Van Helsing raised an eyebrow, unsure of what to make of him. She'd never thought of herself as a creature before. Was that how others perceived her?

'I hear you've dabbled in the dark arts yourself,' he said, holding her gaze. 'What do you make of this Hook woman's powers?'

Before Van Helsing could give a reply Alice butted in,

'It's not like she has a chance against her, though. She seems invulnerable, and her hooked hand transforms into a bloody magical cannon. It's mental.'

Van Helsing turned to her assistant, who still held the newspaper and now moved on from the cake slice to a cup of tea on the table next to her.

'Quiet, Alice,' Van Helsing said.

Alice gulped down a mouthful of tea. 'I'm just bein' realistic. If the entire British Army can't stop her, what hope do we bloody have?'

'She's just a simple pirate with a lot of power. So what do we do?' Van Helsing asked.

'Take away her power?' Alice picked up another slice of cake, but stopped before eating it. 'The Amulet that Mr Roxton was hunting!'

With reluctance, Van Helsing turned back to Roxton. 'It's said it can bind the powers of anyone. Is that right?'

'It's just a legend,' Roxton said. 'However, considering what I went through to get it, I don't think we should overlook its potential.'

'It's all we have,' Van Helsing said.

Just then, a slow rumble came from outside.

'But Alice is right,' Roxton said. 'There's no way we can get it close enough. And without the Amulet around her neck, all the bullets in the world won't make a difference. That's if the Amulet works.'

Victor took a step forward. 'Unless I open a portal directly into Buckingham Palace,' he said. 'Thanks to the storm last night, my device should have enough power to manage that.'

The rumble outside had now piqued the interest of everyone in the room, and Van Helsing pulled back the curtain and peered out onto the street.

'What is that?' Alice asked.

'Tanks,' Van Helsing said.

Roxton turned to Alice. 'I thought you said the entire British Army already put up a fight?'

'Well, that's what the paper says. Apparently, she tore 'em apart. Her and that li'l purple fairy.'

Wendy ran into the room, distressed. 'It's all over the wireless. They're headed for the palace. They're going to destroy it.'

Victor headed to the door. 'We need to move—now.'

The others followed him out of the living room, and they headed to the lab.

Victor activated his giant batteries and tinkered with the dials, inputting longitude and latitude.

By the door to the lab stood his wife's cryogenic tank, still bubbling away. Peter's body lay on a stretcher in the lab's walk-in chiller. Victor had called the coroner a few days ago, but with all the panic in London about Hook, he hadn't been available as yet. So here Peter's body stayed. Victor and Wendy both felt keen to bury him.

Roxton walked in, dressed in his hunter's outfit, complete with guns and his fedora hat, and a rifle slung over his shoulder. Alice lifted a couple of worn, dirty battle-axes and handed Van Helsing one.

'Silver edged blade,' Alice said, and then picked up her bag of weapons, which included her trusty croquet mallet. 'And, I'll 'ave the rest with me.'

Van Helsing looked Alice in the eye.

'No. You're sitting this one out.'

'But—' Alice looked angry.

'I mean it, it's too dangerous. When I took you in, I vowed to take care of you. That's what I'm doing.'

'Is it? It sounds like you just don't have any faith in me.'

Victor finished his calculations and pulled the lever, activating the portal device. The neon grid opened up while Roxton, Van Helsing, and Alice watched. The interior of Buckingham Palace came into view.

Roxton looked amazed. 'How did you create this? I can't even begin to comprehend what I'm seeing.'

'The entire universe is energy,' Victor said. 'With the right frequency, and enough power, I managed to punch a hole into the fabric of reality, which revealed this plane of existence. Different frequency settings give a different destination. The grid inside, however, is the real mystery. Nothing about it seems natural.'

'What do you mean by that?'

'I'm fairly certain it's man made. But by whom? I have no idea.'

Van Helsing stepped towards the portal. 'Enough chatter, boys.' She cracked her neck. 'Time is of the essence.' That said, she ran through the portal.

The hunter cocked his rifle and leapt through after her.

Victor powered down the portal device, and Alice grasped hold of the battle-axe in her hand while gritting her teeth. Then she threw the axe as hard as she could at the far wall, slamming it into the brickwork just inches away from the cryogenic tank that held Victor's wife.

Alice gulped and turned to Victor, who couldn't quite contain his fury.

'That's my wife,' he yelled. He stared at Alice until she looked away.

CHAPTER SEVEN

SHOWDOWN AT BUCKINGHAM PALACE

At terrific speed, Van Helsing smashed through the first-floor window and hit the grassy ground of the gardens of Buckingham Palace. Her battle-axe fell beside her and planted into the lawn.

Hook leapt out of the window after her, effortlessly landing on the ground with her cannon arm up and aimed it at the struggling Van Helsing, who still sat trying to gather her senses.

Hook fired an energy blast, and Van Helsing managed to roll out of the way. The blast sent grass and dirt flying around her, but before Hook could fire again, Roxton had jumped onto her back, struggling to put the Amulet around her neck.

Hook shook off the burly man and threw him to the ground, then turned to see Van Helsing grabbing her battle-axe. With a mighty yell, she threw it at Hook, but the wily pirate caught the flying blade and used it to deflect the onslaught of bullets from Roxton's twin Colts as they fired at her body.

Sparks flew off the blade when the projectiles hit, and Roxton soon found his guns out of ammo. Hook flung the axe at him, and it slammed into the ground in between his legs, the edge of the blade nestling his crotch. Roxton shouted at Van Helsing and threw the Amulet to her.

Hook fired her cannon at the vampire hunter, who charged towards her. With an impressive display of acrobatics, Van Helsing cartwheeled out of the way of Hook's attack.

The entire city had watched the tanks head towards Buckingham Palace and drive towards the gates. The radio had mentioned that the Prime Minister had consulted with the King, and they'd decided that they would use the full force of their military might against Hook, even if that meant destroying the palace.

Roxton had managed to reload his weapons and once again fired at Hook, who simply held up her hand and stopped the bullets in mid air. He continued firing, wanting her looking in his direction so Van Helsing could come up behind her.

As soon as the Van Helsing placed the Amulet

around Hook's neck, a glowing aura emanated from her body and faded away into the ether. Van Helsing balled her fist and, using all her strength, punched Hook in the stomach. There was a risk the Amulet wouldn't work. Her entire fist may end up mangled and crushed, as though punching a brick wall, but she gave it everything she had.

Hook fell to the ground, struggling to breathe, and held her stomach while making gasping noises like a dying bear. Van Helsing grabbed her by her luscious red hair and lifted her to her feet. Another crack to the face sent her stumbling to Roxton, who pushed his shoulder into her middle and lifted her up. He ran toward the palace and threw her through one of the glass windows.

She landed in a shower of glass and wood, trying to raise her cannon arm, but the weapon proved useless.

Van Helsing and Roxton approached. The sounds of the tanks getting into position at the front of the building reached them.

'Stop playing with her and knock her out,' Van Helsing said. 'We have no time. The tanks will fire at any second.'

'Why don't you use one of those magic spells that you like writing about so much?' he said.

Roxton climbed into the palace. Hook ran away and pulled the Amulet from around her neck. Hands a blur of speed, he drew his gun and fired. The bullets ripped through her body and embedded in the elegant portrait behind her. Hook dropped to the floor like a chunk of wet meat, and the Amulet fell from her hand and hit the floor next to her.

Roxton ran toward the body, keeping his gun trained on the downed pirate. The aura he had seen disappear from her body glowed into life once more. The blood surrounding her motionless figure slunk back into the gaping bullet wounds in her flesh and, within moments, Hook's eyes opened and she catapulted upright, her eyes glowing the same red as her buoyant hair. She raised her cannon, and the inside of the turret glowed a shimmering purple.

'That hurt,' she said and blasted an almighty beam of energy at Roxton, narrowly missing him and destroying the wall beside him, which brought the entire ceiling down on top of him.

Van Helsing stepped into the palace through the shattered window. Hook launched herself through the corridor and into the vampire hunter.

Just outside the windows they saw the soldiers make their attack on the palace as they drove their tanks through the front gate, knocking them over with force. They came to a halt in the front courtyard. The turrets of the tanks aimed directly at the front of the building.

Van Helsing and Hook emerged at high speed from the front door, which exploded into pieces.

They hit the ground hard with Hook's force field making a long, gravelly streak behind them when they skidded along the concrete.

The military leaders shouted to hold fire, and the soldiers watched as Hook got to her feet and looked down at the battered woman beneath her. Her cannon powered up again, and this time she wouldn't miss.

It started as a light in the corner of her eye. Something to ignore. Something she needn't be distracted by. But the light moved, and in Hook's experience, when a tiny little light heads your way, it's never something to ignore.

Hook turned her head and looked up at the stars. Sure enough, one of them fell. Fell at quite a pace, and the more she stared, the more she felt sure the star glowed green in colour.

She raised her cannon, but the tiny, green sparkling light travelled so fast it had already hit her jaw at three times the sound of speed. The punch came harder than any of the humans could manage and dazed Hook for a while; long enough for the little green light to circle back and strike her in the stomach, and then uppercut her jaw once more. Hook stumbled backwards; nearly losing consciousness when the tiny shimmering spark flew up to the sky and, in a blast of bright green energy, grew a hundred times larger.

———

Roxton pushed the plaster and lumber off his

bruised body and staggered to the destroyed front door.

Tinker Bell concentrated all her energy into her hands and fired an almighty blast of energy at the waning villain. The bright green beam of electrical discharge hit Hook square in the chest and she fell back on the ground, her clothes smoking as she lay still, defeated.

Roxton watched as Tink fluttered her glowing green plasma wings in the sky above the fallen Hook. They let out a hum he'd never heard before, like trapped energy compressed under pressure. She fell from the sky with elegance and landed on one knee in the middle of the courtyard.

Van Helsing had come to. The fairy's wings retracted into her back, and she looked up at both hunters.

'Where's Peter?' she asked with a stern look on her face. A blast of air blew her bright blonde fringe across her face, which exposed her half-shaved head.

A portal opened up and, inside, through the neon grid, stood Victor with his hand on the lever of his equipment.

'Through here. Bring Hook through here, quick,' he said.

CHAPTER EIGHT

CAGED

Victor knocked on the door of the spare room where Wendy had shut herself in. She had been crying for an hour. Victor opened the bedroom door and walked in slowly. 'Wendy,' he said in a soft voice. 'Someone here to see you.'

She sat up when Victor opened the door wide and let in Tink. Wendy's face lit up when she saw the welcoming look on her face. 'Tinker Bell!'

'Wendy!' She ran towards her, giving her a huge hug.

Wendy wrapped her arms around the little fairy's scant armour and squeezed her so tightly. 'It's good to see you.'

Victor walked across the landing and, through the windows, could see Alice wandering around outside. He felt awful about shouting at her earlier. Not many people got to see that side of him. He'd been looking at Alice's miniaturization suit while Van Helsing and Roxton had been fighting Hook, and thought he might have come up with a solution. Maybe Alice needed some good news.

He headed outside, into the back garden, and walked up to her. 'You can see the entire Milky Way on a clear night,' he said. 'Not tonight, though; looks like there's going to be another thunderstorm.'

'I quite like the thunder, actually,' Alice said.

'Many people do.'

'I'm sorry about throwing the axe, Doctor.'

'No, no, I'm sorry. I shouldn't have shouted. I could see you were annoyed. I probably only made you feel worse.'

'Van Helsing was the one who made me feel bad,' Alice said. 'She don't realise I'm a grown up at all. Sometimes I wish I was still in that asylum. Everything was so simple.'

Victor looked up into the sky. 'You know ... no one knows just how big the universe is. It's entirely possible that it just goes on forever. And if that's the case, and there's an infinite amount of matter out there, it means all those atoms can only arrange themselves in a finite number of ways.'

Alice looked up at the sky and over at Victor. 'You

know what, sometimes you talk, and I hear the words but understand absolutely nothing.' Confusion clouded her features.

'It means that somewhere out there, there's another Earth. With another Alice. And she is still in that asylum.'

Alice looked back out to the sky, looking right where Victor pointed.

'Now, who do you think has it better?' he asked. Then he left a pause, seeing Alice had fallen deep into thought over his words. 'Oh, and I think I managed to fix that suit of yours. After we've dealt with Hook, maybe we can see about getting it working?'

Victor left her looking up at the sky and walked back into the house.

———

Tink and Wendy sat together in the bedroom. Tink asked about Peter, and Wendy thought about how she could avoid it or change the subject. She had spent the last few days without him, but couldn't keep the thought of him being dead out of her mind.

'How did Hook get here?' Tink asked. 'She's ripped Neverland apart, and I'm afraid she'll do the same to London.'

'We opened a portal ... looking for you,' Wendy said.

'Well, where's Peter? Maybe together we can stop

her.'

'P-P-Peter ...' Wendy struggled to say the words. Teeth gritted, she was determined just to say it. Say it and get it out there and done with. 'Peter tried ... she killed him.'

A cascade of silent tears rolled down her cheeks yet again, but Tink didn't look upset. No, she looked angry.

'I'll kill her.' Tink balled her fist. 'Where's his body?'

From inside her cage, Hook stared at the body in the chiller, and then looked over at the bubbling cylinder that contained the beautiful woman, wrapped in bandages. She took in all the electronic devices and machinery in the lab and tried to ignore the condemning stares from Roxton and Van Helsing as she gripped onto the bars.

In front of her face dangled the Amulet, now attached to the front of the cage—the small prison cell keeping her powerless. The one thing that fully caught her eye was the device that opened up that hole into Neverland. The portal projector sat on a table in the middle of the lab. Its potential limitless.

Victor walked in just as Van Helsing took off her coat and saw Alice's bag of weaponry leaning against the wall.

'Where's Alice?' she asked.

Victor stood and watched Hook, who had refused to say anything since she'd awoken in the cage. All she did was watch.

'She's outside, sulking,' Victor said. 'You made the right choice, though.'

'Did I?' Van Helsing asked. 'Are we even making the right choice now? Why did we bring her back here? The authorities could have taken her.'

'I thought it would be safer this way,' Victor said. 'We have her contained, and that's all that matters. Also, you said there was no sign of that fairy she was with?'

Roxton took off his hat and took a seat. 'Not that we saw. I'm not sure we'd have made it back if we'd had to contend with her as well.'

'Speak for yourself,' Van Helsing said. 'Besides, we failed. We'd both be dead, and Buckingham Palace surely destroyed if it wasn't for—'

Tinker Bell burst through the lab doors and marched over to Hook's cage. 'Let her out, I want her face caved in.'

Victor grabbed Tink by the arm, keeping her from ripping the cage door off. 'Whoa, don't touch the cage. That Amulet is the only thing keeping her powers contained.'

'You can't send her back to Neverland.' Tink pushed Victor away. 'She's ravaged it. We must kill her while we can.'

Wendy rushed in while Victor once again grabbed Tink and kept her away from the cage.

'Nobody is killing anyone,' Victor said. 'Wendy, get her out. Everyone, out.'

Wendy and Van Helsing ushered Tink out of the lab.

Roxton got up and grabbed his hat. 'Are you all right there, Victor?' he asked.

'I'll be fine.'

Roxton walked out. Victor leant on the table in the middle of his lab, next to the portal device.

Behind him, Hook bit her lip and glanced once more at the woman in the tank of bubbling liquid. 'This laboratory of yours is impressive,' she said. 'Harnessing such power ... but is the travelling device the only contraption you've used it for?'

Victor kept his head low, not bothering to look back at her. 'My experiments are none of your concern.'

'The woman,' Hook said. 'Was she your wife?'

Victor turned his head slightly, and his rage showed. 'Do. Not. Even. Speak. Of. Her.'

'Now I understand. You would use this power to bring her back from the dead.'

Victor looked over at his wife. Hook followed his gaze. The woman's hair danced around her shoulders as the bubbles in the cryogenic liquid rose up past her peaceful face.

'It doesn't work,' he said. 'Such a thing, I fear, is impossible.'

Hook took a moment, revelling in the silence before uttering her next four words. 'Was it her heart?'

Victor turned around and walked up to the cage, his eyes wide open, astonished that she would have any knowledge of his work. 'How did you know that?'

'It couldn't take the energy you pumped into her corpse, could it?'

'As I said ... it is impossible.'

'Your experiment will work,' Hook said.

Victor moved even closer to the bars of the cage. Hook had him; he didn't care who she was; if she had any kind of knowledge or if her powers could somehow help, he would be willing to listen.

'Tell me how,' he said.

Hook took a deep breath and shook her long, cascading red hair away from her shoulders. She looked Victor deep in the eyes and eased forward, so her nose almost touched the bars of the cage. 'No.'

Victor slammed his hands into the cage, grabbed the bars, and shook the entire structure, hard. Then yelled, 'Tell me.'

Hook stood back and leant against the back of the cage. 'A bargain. I tell you how, and you open that hole back to Neverland. You'll never see me again. I'll surely die if I stay here.'

'Send you back to Neverland? I'd be condemning it.'

'Tinker Bell fights me because she fears change. They all refuse to grow up. But I changed that. I forced them to.'

'You're a monster.'

'Perhaps.' Hook could see the desperation in Victor's eyes and knew exactly what buttons to push. In much the same way as she had gained control of the entire pirate fleet in Neverland, she was now about to gain control of Victor Frankenstein and his machine. 'You must think on what you really care about. Do you care about an island a world away? Do you care so much what others think? What have you been striving to achieve for so long?'

Victor looked over at his wife. Would he do it? Betray his friends to bring back his wife?

After a full thirty seconds of deliberation, he said, 'Okay, I'll do it.'

'One more thing,' Hook said.

'What?'

She loved to play, and Victor made a great, shiny new toy. Hook really should let Victor get on, but she couldn't help but see just how far she could push him. It was never about the endgame. Maybe Peter Pan had been correct; it was about the playing. And, right now, Hook was having the most fun she'd had in a while.

'A kiss,' she said and moved back towards the front of the cage, putting on her most innocent face. Never had she witnessed such love and devotion. She didn't understand it. Although she'd heard stories of love, and many inhabitants of Neverland had stories of love and loss before they found themselves there, she'd never felt it and likely never would. So, just to taste it once, to sample it from this man's lips, would be intriguing to her.

Victor hesitated slightly but made his way to the bars. His Adam's apple bobbed in a gulp when he looked down at Hook's full lips. Hook reached out through the bars and grabbed his shirt. Then she pulled him closer, so his body squished against the metal, and looked at Victor's eyes. While she did so, she placed something in his hand.

Victor looked down at it. A thimble. Hook pushed him away from the cage.

'Funny,' he said.

'Are you sure it's your wife you want?' Who needed a kiss? Love seemed overrated anyway, she thought.

'Now tell me how I bring my wife back. How do I make it work?'

Hook smiled, relaxed, and glanced over at the chiller at the far end of the lab. 'You replace her heart ... with Peter's.'

RICK BUSH

CHAPTER NINE

THE HEART OF THE MATTER

Above Frankenstein Manor, lightning flew across the cloudy night sky and, for a moment, lit up the intimidating house.

Van Helsing walked out into the back garden and joined Alice, who stood and stared up at the sky. 'It's starting to rain. Come back inside.'

Alice continued to look up at the sky, waiting for another lightning bolt. 'All you bloody do is tell me what I should be doing. How about letting me make my own decisions?'

'It's not that I don't think you can. I care about you. I brought you into this crazy world of ours and I couldn't bear it if something were to happen. Because it would be my fault.'

Alice turned to face her mentor. 'You didn't force me to fight vampires. I wanted to learn. *I wanted this*. I'm not saying you have to let me go out there and fight demonic forces alone; I'm just saying that ... oh bloody hell, I don't know what I'm saying.'

Van Helsing knew what she meant and had to stop herself from apologising to her young assistant. She could see the path that would take them down. Alice would be happy but careless. She'd think too much of herself and, with that pride, would come the fall. Though it would hurt Alice and herself, Van Helsing knew the right course of action. 'I understand, Alice, I do. But you're sixteen-years-old and it's only a few months since you left the asylum.'

'What's that got to do with anything?' Alice scrunched up her brow.

Van Helsing had offended her. She stuck her chest out and stood as tall as she could, trying to dwarf Alice below her. 'What we have is not a partnership. You are my apprentice, and I make the rules. So, when I say fight, you fight. And when I say stay at home, you stay at home. Or you can go back to wandering around the dark alleys begging for food.'

Alice shook her head and snorted in disbelief, and then ran back towards the house. Another lightning strike in the clouds above lit up the garden. Van Helsing looked up and stared into the night sky.

Victor pulled his black rubber apron over his sweaty brow and fastened it. Then he locked the door to the laboratory and pulled up his surgical mask with his gloved hands. The two bodies placed side by side on the tables in the centre of the lab gave him chills. A moment of hesitation drifted over him, but—too late now. Slowly, he walked over to his trolley of tools and wheeled it over to Peter's body.

Hook watched from her cage while Victor unzipped Peter's green-and-black leather vest, which exposed his chest, and pulled out a scalpel. He hesitated once more and took a moment to look at Elizabeth, who lay next to Peter. He had become so used to seeing Elizabeth with her metallic upgrades, that the cybernetic pistons and technology erupting from her biceps and thighs seemed perfectly at home in his laboratory. Would it be different outside? Could they be normal again? They used to have dinner parties where Elizabeth would invite the cream of London socialites to gather and talk. He longed for those days once more; perhaps the way she looked now would be a rather interesting talking point? How could anyone refuse a conversation about the genius internal workings of her bionic protrusions?

Victor turned his attention back to Peter's chest and made his first incision. He peeled back the skin around the sternum until he'd exposed the rib cage. The lack of muscles in that location made it ideal for surgery. He clipped the skin back so it stayed open, and then picked up the electric saw. He noticed Hook smirk when the blade dug into Peter's bones, slashing specks of blood over Victor's face.

Once he'd sawed the rib cage lengthways through the sternum, Victor put down the saw and picked up the rib spreaders. The rib cage being quite flexible, Victor managed to pull the ribs apart with relative ease.

For the next few minutes, Victor took his time cutting the coronary arteries around the heart until it came free from Peter's body. With gentle hands, he lifted it up and, for a moment, could have sworn he saw it glimmer a bright green. He placed it in a bowl and headed over to Elizabeth.

A year ago, after his experiment's final failure, he'd sealed her chest. Her heart had been utterly destroyed, as had most of her rib cage. He'd put her back together as best he could, using metal parts to do the job of her bones. Now, he opened her up once again and exposed his handiwork. He needed no saw with Elizabeth, as he'd made sure he would always be able to upgrade and repair her as needed. With a slide of a panel on her breastplate, the entire metal ribcage opened like a welcoming flower, beckoning the sunlight. Victor lowered in the heart, and then sewed the arteries together.

———

Wendy and Tinker Bell joined Van Helsing and Roxton in the living room.

'Is Victor still in the lab?' Wendy asked.

'I assume so,' Roxton said. 'Complicated man, isn't he?'

Tink looked frustrated. 'Are we just keeping Hook locked up forever? Shouldn't we notify someone? Oh, this is ridiculous; I'm going to talk to him.' She stormed toward the door on the far side of the room.

Behind her, Roxton said to Van Helsing, 'Feisty thing, isn't she?' Then he followed her to the lab.

Tink tried the door handle but found the door locked. 'Frankenstein? Let me in.'

Roxton moved past Tink and tried the door himself, as though the diminutive pixie may be too weak to open such a large and foreboding door. He, too, found it locked.

Van Helsing rushed past the two of them. She thumped on the door as Tink and the others looked on. 'Victor? What are you doing in there?' She turned back to the others. 'I think we need to get this door open.'

Roxton took a few steps back and prepared to charge at it. Tink kicked the door wide open, and after a brief glance at Roxton, she marched inside the lab with everyone else behind her.

Victor stood by the lever, waiting for the storm to power his machines. In front of him lay his wife, hooked up to the electrodes on the table where the portal device once stood, and next to her on an operating table lay Peter with his chest wide open. The empty gaping hole in his front, in plain view for all to see. Victor hadn't even bothered taking out the rib spreaders.

Wendy stared at Peter's body in utter disgust, unable to even look at Victor, then ran out of the room.

Before Tink could make her way to Victor and knock him out, a great crash of thunder and lightning hit the antenna on the roof, and Victor's machines roared into life.

Victor pulled the lever. An insane amount of electricity poured into Elizabeth's body, which made her spasm and jolt. The glass bulbs on Victor's machines shone brightly and then burst, sending particles of glass over the floor. The lights in the lab flickered on and off before also exploding, and sent a spray of glass down on everyone's heads. Victor kept his eyes on the dials, and when they hit a certain level, he threw the lever back, cutting off the power.

Elizabeth sat bolt upright and screamed.

She screamed.

And screamed.

And screamed.

When she stopped, everyone stood still, staring at this woman covered in bandages with metal parts piercing her arms and legs.

'She's alive,' Victor whispered. Elizabeth stared into nothingness, and he dashed to her side.

'Elizabeth, are you all right?' he asked.

His wife turned to him and her blank face morphed to one of anger and confusion. She brought her almighty metallic arm up and slammed it into Victor, sending him sprawling onto Peter's body, and knocking him to the ground, where he ended up falling on top the surgical tools.

Awkwardly, Elizabeth got off the table and pulled off the electrodes attached to her body. She then grabbed the heavy table and lifted it clean off the ground, toppling it over. It came to rest right next to the portal device.

Hook watched with glee as Frankenstein's wife made her way over to him. He still lay on the ground amongst his tools.

Van Helsing ran after her and leapt on her back.

'No, don't hurt her,' Victor yelled.

Roxton pulled out his guns. 'Which one are you talking to?'

Elizabeth spun Van Helsing around and slammed her against Hook's cage with an almighty thump. Van Helsing fell to the ground, as did the Amulet.

While Frankenstein's league fought Elizabeth, Hook opened the door of her cage and stepped out of her prison. Her powers returned. She transformed her hook into the cannon and aimed it at the Amulet, which lay on the ground. Something stopped her from destroying it, though. Instead, she raised her hand and the Amulet floated up to her eye height. From where did its power come? The energy inside it spoke to her. She held it in her hand, careful not to wrap it around her, and—all of a sudden—she perceived its entire history and the deadly secret that it contained. She put it in her pocket and walked over to the portal device.

Tink unloaded her green energy beam from her hands and hit Elizabeth in the chest. It just seemed to anger her more and she slapped Tink across the lab, smashing the cryogenic tank that had recently housed Elizabeth's preserved body.

The cooling liquid spread out on the laboratory floor as Hook picked up the portal device.

'She's got your machine, Frankenstein,' Roxton said. He fired at her. With a simple gesture, she sent the bullets flying back towards him, and they pinged into the walls around him as he hit the floor.

Hook smirked and flew straight up through the ceiling, sending a pile of debris to the ground. From there, she watched as the scene of mayhem continued to unfold.

Elizabeth turned her attention to Van Helsing, who struggled to get up off the ground. She raised her fist to smash her face in but an immense explosive beam of energy from Tinker Bell's gun hit her, propelling her into the air and through the laboratory window.

Elizabeth hit the grass in the back garden with a thump, slowly picked herself up, and moved off, tearing through the fence at the rear and toward the town beyond.

Tink helped Van Helsing up and holstered her sidearm.

'Quite the warrior, little fairy,' Van Helsing said.

'I can hold my own.' She turned her attention to Peter's body, which now lay on the floor, looking a mess. Tink looked at Victor, who got to his feet. 'You used his body?'

'I ... I had to try.'

'Congratulations,' Van Helsing said. 'I hope it was worth it.'

Tink walked right up to his face and yelled, 'You diabolical man. How dare you—you had no right. No right!'

'It was the only way to—'

'I should fly you to the heavens and drop you.'

Van Helsing took her by the arm and led her toward the exit.

'You lost some friends today, Victor,' Van Helsing said. Then they left him alone with Roxton.

Victor crossed to the knocked-over table. Roxton walked up to him and helped him lift Peter's body back on it. 'Your wife,' Roxton said. 'Was she always that angry?'

'I had no idea if it would work at all. I love my wife, Mr Roxton. I would have done anything to get her back.'

Roxton grabbed his hat from the floor. 'Well, we can't have her running amok.' He placed the hat on his head. 'I'll see if I can track her down.'

'That would be appreciated.' Victor watched as Roxton left the room. For the moment, he'd forgotten all about Hook. All he wanted was not to be alone again, and through his actions he now felt more alone than ever.

CHAPTER TEN

BRIDE OF FRANKENSTEIN

Van Helsing led Tink into the living room. The little fairy walked into the room with brisk, agitated steps.

'Who is this man?' she said. 'He opens a portal to my home and releases all manner of terror on this world. He gets my best friend killed, and then desecrates his body for his selfish purposes.'

Van Helsing could see her point. Victor was far from the norm, but she'd never thought he would pull his friend's heart out and attach it to his dead wife's corpse. Just thinking it through in her mind felt surreal. But this was the man who could help them catch Hook once and for all and save the world. 'He's complicated,' she said.

If they were going to have any chance of fighting Hook, it would have to be together. 'But sometimes he's quite brilliant.'

She placed a hand on Tink's shoulder, which caused the fairy to flinch. Her bright glowing wings shot out of her back and Tink lifted off the ground in full battle mode, holding up her glowing fist. Her eyes glowed a sparkly red colour as if she couldn't contain her anger.

'Back off. You don't want to mess with a fairy.'

In an attempt to calm things down, Van Helsing said, 'Because you can hold your own.'

'Damn straight I can.' Tink lowered her fist and sank back to the floor, deactivating her wings. 'I should leave this place. Go home. Try rebuilding our world now she's not there.'

Van Helsing could see the reasoning. Why bother fighting Hook when she no longer posed a threat to Neverland? 'Stay and fight with us. Hook has Victor's portal device. She'll only cause more suffering to both our worlds. And, maybe together ...'

Tink turned away and looked out of the window. 'I don't particularly want to work in a team. In Neverland, I watched so many of my friends die. I've lost too much.'

Van Helsing walked up behind her, cautious; this little fairy was small but feisty. A punch from her could knock her head clean off. 'I think we're very much alike. Together, we can save this world. And yours.' She held out her hand, and Tink hesitated slightly before grasping it. 'You saved my life back there. I will return the favour. That's a promise.'

Tink said, 'And what exactly do we do with Hook when we find her?'

'Oh, that's easy.' Van Helsing smiled. 'We kill the harpy.'

Roxton stood in the kitchen with his two suitcases wide open, spread out on the table. Inside them lay an array of weaponry and hunting paraphernalia. He loaded a few extra magazines for his Colts and picked up the rifle and a long whip.

Alice walked into the room, now wearing her blue overalls with the electrodes all over them. She'd added a pair of white leather boots and gloves to the outfit and had taken Victor's protective goggles, which she wore around her neck.

'Just what do you think you're doing?' Roxton asked.

Alice paused and tried not to frown. 'Helping you get Doctor Frankenstein's wife back.'

'And what are you wearing, exactly?'

'It's my miniaturisation suit. Doctor Frankenstein fixed it so now I should be able to shrink down to a tiny size.' Alice looked proud of her new uniform.

'Right. And how is being small going to help us

catch Mrs Frankenstein?'

Alice didn't feel too sure. All she knew was that she had a power—an ability—and she wanted to show Van Helsing that she didn't need mothering. 'Well, if I need to get into small places ... I can ... get ... in them ...' Alice wondered just how she was supposed to implement this strange power.

Roxton picked up his rifle and handed it to Alice. 'Here, you hold this. And some of this ammunition. Maybe we can make you useful after all, hmm?'

Roxton walked out, and even though Alice found the situation familiar, she felt excited to be allowed to be going on a mission. If only she could work out how to use her suit. Frankenstein had said that the power came from her. That she made it happen. The suit just amplified it. Just a matter of concentrating, she supposed, as was always the way with these sorts of things.

Roxton and Alice walked to the back of the garden and the rain splattered down on them. The storm had subsided but the clouds were full to bursting. Roxton walked up to the broken fence, which surrounded Frankenstein's land.

'I don't think tracking her is going to be too difficult,' he said.

It wasn't the tracking that had him worried, though.

To subdue Elizabeth would be the awkward part. He could put a bullet through her brain with no problem, but bringing her back alive meant being stealthy and taking her by surprise. She had such intense strength—and that anger? What had Frankenstein done to her mind? He guessed if he'd been dead for a couple of years, he'd probably be a little out of sorts too.

Alice followed Roxton through the green wooded area at the back of Frankenstein Manor until they reached a road. No sign of Elizabeth. Roxton walked up to a broken wooden gate and tore off a section of bandage that had obviously gotten caught and ripped from her body.

At that point, they heard the scream. It seemed to come from the main road not far from where they stood.

'This way, she's over there.' Alice ran towards the commotion.

Roxton caught up with her and grabbed her arm. 'Not so loud. We need to sneak up on her. If she's startled, she could tear the whole street apart.'

The two of them made their way to the street, where Elizabeth stood in the middle of the road, looking confused. Roxton knelt down and glanced at Alice.

'The rifle,' he said.

'We can't kill her,' Alice said but handed over the rifle.

'We're not killing her. I loaded the rifle with darts. Enough to knock out a giant ape—should be enough to put her to sleep.' Roxton aimed the gun at Elizabeth.

'Shouldn't we try and talk to her first?' Alice asked.

Roxton had the robotic woman in his sights. He could take her out right now and that would be it. What had him less sure was what the dart would do to her. Only parts of her remained human. What if he gave her too much dosage? It could kill her. But then, could he kill something already dead?

Roxton lowered the gun and sighed. He handed the rifle back to Alice and walked out into the street. At this late hour, very few cars were on the road. The disturbance had brought what little traffic there was to a standstill. The more time she stayed out there, the more innocent bystanders would be in danger.

'Mrs Frankenstein?' Roxton approached at a slow pace. 'Elizabeth Frankenstein?'

She turned around and looked him straight in the eye. When she spoke, her words sounded slurred and strained, like she had to learn to communicate all over again.

'I ... don't .... know you,' she said, tilting her head to one side like a confused puppy.

This was good. Maybe Alice had it right. If he could reason with her, he may be able to simply walk her back to Frankenstein, unhurt.

'I know you're angry,' Roxton said. 'And confused. I think you should just come with me.'

Elizabeth edged toward Roxton. If not for the car

horn, everything would have been fine.

Thomas Middleton was in a hurry—his wife was in labour—and he'd been away on a business trip in Manchester. The baby probably wouldn't come for a few hours, and that should give him time enough to drive down and be there for the birth of his first child. He only had a couple of miles to go now; he would make it. He would be the hero, arriving on time to see his wife's smiling, proud face. The affair he'd had last year would be all but forgotten and forgiven. If only he could get there in time.

The two cars ahead of Mr Middleton slowed to a halt at the strange sight. And an onslaught of rain poured down onto the roads, and all of this forced him to slam on the brakes.

It wasn't every day that a huge cyborg woman stopped traffic, and he could completely understand the logic of slowing down and taking a look. Even Thomas felt rather intrigued by the sight of it, but only for approximately four seconds, by which time he felt he'd seen all that was to be seen and gleaned all there was to be gleaned by the vision of the android female striding around in the middle of the road just after midnight.

The little traffic on the road had now built up on both sides. If only the cars would have pulled over slightly, he may have been able to drive past them and carry on his journey. But they hadn't, and he got stuck, and now some guy in a hat was trying to talk to the strange woman. He'd had enough; he needed to get to the hospital right now. He needed the cars to pull over. He needed that woman to get out of his damn way.

He pushed his hand down on the horn for a good three seconds. Another good three seconds had elapsed before he realised his action had been a colossal mistake.

The long, loud honk startled Elizabeth, and she slammed her hand down on the nearest car. The entire bonnet caved in and the front windscreen smashed, sending a spray of glass over the street, and exposing the driver behind the wheel.

Elizabeth raised her fist once more. Alice watched as Roxton pulled out his whip, and with a sharp crack, had the end of it wrapped around her wrist. The driver ran from the car as Elizabeth grabbed the leather whip and yanked Roxton off his feet and then threw him to the glass-covered ground.

'Leave ... me ... alone,' she said as she picked him up and threw him over the first two cars in front of her and into the windscreen of Thomas Middleton's vehicle.

Roxton pulled himself out of the wreckage and sat upright, looking over at Alice at the far end of the street, who still had hold of his rifle.

'Alice,' he shouted. 'Take the shot. Take her down.'

She had never fired a gun before but had seen plenty of action heroes do it at the pictures. This was her moment. No longer sitting on the sidelines, she would be integral to the capture of Mrs Frankenstein. This was how she wished Van Helsing would treat her—like a partner.

Gunstock to her shoulder, she lifted the heavy weapon so it aimed at Elizabeth, who had picked up the first car and now lifted it above her head.

Roxton shouted at her again, but Alice couldn't keep the gun still—it shook and waved all over the place. She held her breath and steadied the gun as much as she could. Her heart beat so fast; a miss could mean the death of Roxton and several bystanders.

The gun seemed to get lighter in her hands while she concentrated, but as she looked through the sights, she could see Mrs Frankenstein get further and further away. Her whole vision changed and her body felt odd. The gun now felt as light as a feather. Unfortunately, so did she.

━━━

Van Helsing walked out of Alice's room and into Wendy's, where Tink sat comforting her.

'You haven't seen Alice anywhere, have you?' she asked.

Wendy shook her teary-eyed head, and Van Helsing hurried downstairs. In the kitchen, she found Alice's weapon bag leant next to Roxton's suitcases of weaponry and hunting gear. She had searched the entire house and garden and couldn't find her anywhere. Though she loathed to talk to him right now, Van Helsing made her way into Victor's lab, where she found him tidying up the mess, and trying to lift the slate table that his wife had so easily toppled over.

'Victor,' she said. 'Have you seen Alice? I can't find her anywhere. I think she must be with Roxton.'

Victor gave up on moving the slab and stood up straight. 'She's with Roxton? He's off looking for Elizabeth.' He dashed over to the desk where he'd been working on Alice's shrinking suit. It had gone.

'She's taken her suit,' he said in a panic. 'But it wasn't ready. I found a flaw I hadn't fixed yet.'

'What flaw?' Van Helsing asked with a frown.

'If she manages to shrink her body and anything else she's touching, she can only stay like that for about a minute before ...' He stopped talking, not wanting even to suggest the consequences.

'Before what, Victor?'

'The electromagnetic force will spring back to normal. But an unprocessed reversion to full size would rip the very bonds that hold her atoms together.'

'What does that mean?' Van Helsing walked toward him, serious as hell. 'In plain English. Or Dutch. I'm fluent in both.'

'She'll explode.'

CHAPTER ELEVEN

DRINK ME

Roxton watched in astonishment as Alice disappeared, along with his rifle.

Elizabeth threw the car she had been lifting above her head, and Roxton leapt to the ground as it smashed into Thomas Middleton's vehicle and crushed the man to death.

He had no choice; Roxton pulled his two Colt 1911s from his holsters and trained them on Elizabeth. Maybe if he could hit the metal parts, he could stop her from using her arms. He fired, and Elizabeth managed to deflect the bullets with her metal wrists.

'You ... cannot ... stop me ...' she said and beat her fists into the wet ground, cracking the tarmac and knocking Roxton off his feet. As Roxton regained his feet, she leapt into the air and landed with a crunch precisely where he'd stood but a moment ago. Tarmac and rainwater exploded everywhere. He ran towards where Alice had been standing, and then came to an abrupt stop for fear of treading on her.

'Alice? Where are you? I need that rifle.'

Alice looked around at the bizarre, huge world around her. She had been concentrating on aiming the rifle, not shrinking to this size. But at least she now knew for certain she could control it. Just a matter of concentrating on enlarging. Her concentration, however, got interrupted by Roxton's gigantic body falling right next to her on top of the bag of weapons she had put down. Elizabeth pounced on top of him and grabbed him by the throat.

Alice stumbled into a puddle and dropped the rifle. The surge of water on the ground swept her off her feet and, all at once, she found herself being taken for a ride along the gutter.

Alice travelled directly underneath Roxton, who fired his gun at Elizabeth's shoulder, which only seemed to anger her even more, but it gave Roxton the chance to free himself from her vice-like clutches and grab his bag of weaponry.

He pulled out the croquet mallet that Alice had insisted on bringing and swung it at Elizabeth's face, but it didn't connect. She managed to catch it and wrench it out of his fists. Then she threw it across the street.

The drain came up fast. Alice was in trouble. She only had a few seconds before she would plummet into the sewers below.

As soon as Alice got far enough away, her influence on the rifle subsided, and it sprang back to its full size.

The gun burst into life beside Roxton, and he grabbed it. Elizabeth took hold of Roxton, lifted him over her head, and proceeded to throw him into the wreckage of cars. The rifle landed on the top of the destroyed vehicles, and Roxton slid off and hit the ground. Elizabeth advanced on him, walking away from Alice, who still struggle-swam in the gutter.

Alice took a deep breath and sank under the water. She closed her eyes tight and tried to forget where she was and how small she had become. All she thought about was growing. She hit the side of the drain cover and bashed her head hard against the metal structure. With a gasp, she reached out and managed to hold onto the edge—the only thing that kept her from falling into the drain. Her fingers hurt, but she had to concentrate. She closed her eyes and blocked out everything. The sounds of fighting drifted away. The sounds of screaming people faded. Alice concentrated on the water —the epic onslaught of rushing water that brushed her ears. It no longer felt like a distraction. It felt like a comfort.

Alice grew. Against the torrent of water, she pulled

herself up out of the drain. The bigger she got, the easier she found it until she climbed free of her death trap and became full size once more, although soaking wet.

Roxton scrambled up the tower of motorcars and reached the rifle. He stood atop the smoking vehicles and aimed the gun at Elizabeth, who came in for the kill. He fired, hitting her square in the neck. The dart punctured her skin and its sedating properties flooded into her bloodstream. She reached the cars, and Roxton reloaded the rifle at speed. It wasn't needed, though, and Elizabeth's cumbersome body fell to the ground, where it slumped against the wreckage.

Roxton looked over at Alice, whose once-luscious hair now stuck to her face. Water dripped off her nose. He rested the rifle on his shoulder, looking proud. 'Well, that wasn't such a chore now, was it?'

Van Helsing and Victor arrived on the street. Traffic had started to move, as the police cornered off Elizabeth's slumbering body and directed the cars around it.

Van Helsing ran up to Alice. 'What the hell did you think you were doing?'

Alice looked solemn; she had tried to help but only ended up putting herself in danger. Was Van Helsing right? Maybe she should stay on the sidelines and be a sidekick. Her shrinking powers didn't seem to be any use at all.

'Ah, leave her alone.' Roxton approached them. 'She wanted to help. She makes a heck of a distraction, too.'

Van Helsing lashed out and collided her fist into Roxton's jaw. 'How dare you take her out like that. You could have gotten her killed.'

Roxton leapt back in surprise. 'Easy, Miss Punchy. I didn't force her to come along. She insisted.'

Van Helsing turned her attention back to Alice and grabbed her containment suit. 'Why would you just take this thing? Victor said you could explode if you used your powers.'

Alice's eyes widened. 'What do you mean, explode?'

Victor looked away from his sleeping wife and walked up to Van Helsing and Alice. 'I found a fault with the suit. If you stay miniaturized for any longer than a minute, your atoms will end up spread across the entire countryside.'

Alice gulped. 'I guess I should have mentioned I was taking the suit, then.'

At this point, everyone's attention riveted on Elizabeth's body, which had just stood up with a loud whir of servos and pneumatic pistons.

'Jesus, she's awake,' Van Helsing said.

'That's impossible,' Roxton said. 'I put enough juice in her to stop a rampaging rhino.'

Victor took a few steps back. His wife slapped police officers out of her way and tore vehicles apart with her bare hands. Something looked different, though. In the lab, she had been filled with rage, but now she seemed distant. Dead in the eyes. No expression at all. Something he recognised from many restless nights with her. 'She's not awake,' he said. 'Elizabeth sleepwalks. She always has.'

Roxton pulled out his guns. 'Bullets don't tend to do much. How do we take her down if we can't put her down?'

Victor ignored the fact that Roxton had just admitted he'd shot at his wife and tried to think. 'We need Tinker Bell,' he said. 'We need more power.'

Elizabeth picked up another Policeman, who'd just cracked her in the shoulder with his baton. She took hold of him, ripped his body in half, and continued making her way toward a house on the other side of the road. In the window, stood a mother with her two children. Elizabeth approached the door.

'I hate to say it,' Roxton said, loading his rifle with bullets. 'But I think we need to stop her no matter what.' Roxton aimed his gun at Frankenstein's creation.

Victor grabbed the barrel and pushed it to one side. 'No. I'm not about to let you blow her brains out.'

Roxton matched Victor's raised voice. 'What choice do we have?'

'Why don't we just wake her up?' Alice asked.

Victor's frustration transformed to excitement. 'Yes,' he said. 'We just need to wake her. Roxton, what did you use to put her to sleep?'

Roxton, already a few steps ahead of him, rifled through his bag of tricks. He pulled out a smashed syringe, threw it away, and picked out another. This one was intact, but the needle had broken. 'I see what you're saying, Doc. A shot of adrenaline should do the trick, but I'm afraid my toys have been broken. No needle. So, unless you're planning on forcing her to drink it, I'm not sure how we'll get it inside her.'

Alice could see Elizabeth at the front door of the house. Any moment now, she'd break it down, make her way upstairs, and—most likely—murder those children and their mother. Alice had an idea. A ridiculous one, which she was afraid would sound even more ridiculous when she spoke it out loud. Without a better plan coming from anyone else, she decided to blurt it out. 'I have an idea. How about I take the adrenaline, shrink it down with me to a microscopic size, and pour it out inside her body? Then when I leave ...'

'It'll regrow inside her and deliver the dose straight to the bloodstream.' Victor nodded. 'It's brilliant. How do we get you in her body, though?'

Elizabeth slammed against the front door, and the children upstairs cried with intense fear.

Alice pulled a stake out of Van Helsing's belt and held it. 'Van Helsing throws me.'

'This is crazy,' Van Helsing snatched the stake out of

Alice's hand. 'I can't let you do that.'

Elizabeth smashed down the door to the house and took a step inside.

'There's no time,' Victor said. 'Now or never.'

Van Helsing gave in and placed the stake on the ground. Alice grabbed the adrenaline and stood above the wooden weapon.

'Once inside her bloodstream, you won't be able to breathe,' Victor said. 'You'll have to hold your breath until you've released the adrenaline. Then get as close to the skin as possible and increase your size; even if you split her skin open, I can always fix it. The important thing is getting you out in under a minute, understand?'

'Got it,' Alice said, and then she disappeared, shrinking down to the size of a pinhead on the tip of the stake. She grabbed hold of the cumbersome wooden molecules now surrounding her and held tight.

Van Helsing picked up the stake and trained her eye on Elizabeth as she walked into the house. The path of destruction behind her telegraphed what was in store for the family above if they didn't stop her.

Van Helsing sighed and, with a surge of panic, threw the stake across the street and into Elizabeth's shoulder.

The bride of Frankenstein didn't register the pointy wooden implement wedged in her body; she just carried on walking up the stairs as if the screams of the children drew her.

Alice took in a deep breath when she got hurled through the air and suddenly found herself in complete darkness. Inside Elizabeth's body, she couldn't see a thing. After cursing the fact that no one had thought to hand her a lantern, she rummaged around for the syringe of adrenaline that she'd placed in her pocket. About to release the fluid, a rush of blood molecules propelled her backward. Alice had floated into Elizabeth's bloodstream.

Panic would be far from the correct word to use to describe just how worried Alice felt at this point. Out of her mind and off-her-face-on-mescaline-panicked did a better job of describing it. She thrashed her arms around and tried to swim against the tide, but it proved impossible. She still had the syringe grasped in her hand, but the blood flow propelled her along at such intense speeds that she couldn't depress the plunger. All she had to do was put her thumb in place and squeeze, but her panic drained her body of oxygen, and she realised she was about to suffocate to death.

Alice had totally lost track of how long she'd been small but knew she had to release the adrenaline no matter what. She closed her eyes and moved her thumb into position on the plunger. She felt an immense drop as if free-falling and found herself ripped through a tight hole far too small for her. The surrounding flesh ripped, and Alice got pushed through and propelled upward. The syringe fell out of her hand and away from her.

She'd failed. She would explode at the speed of light inside Victor's wife and kill her all over again, and it had all been for nothing.

Damn her suggestions; she couldn't believe she had been so stupid to think she could actually be a hero like Van Helsing or Lord Roxton. Unable to hold her breath any longer, her body convulsed—desperate for air. Maybe if she died, she wouldn't explode. Maybe that would fix everything.

She assumed the others were fighting the huge body she now occupied. Alice also assumed they'd have no luck. Waves of drowsiness overcame her. Alice let go and, expecting to drown, took in an almighty breath.

Alice breathed out that same breath.

She then breathed in another big breath of air.

The lungs—she must be in the lungs. Alice came to rest against a spongy, fleshy surface, and right there, touching her hand, was the syringe. She grabbed it, pushed the tiny tip into the spongy flesh, and released the adrenaline.

Something felt wrong. Her body had gone numb and tense like she'd fallen into a frozen lake. The minute must be up, and she would explode, and could do nothing about it.

Alice couldn't believe that. She wanted to live and make sure no one else got hurt. Still, trapped in a lung that she'd just emptied a whole load of liquid into, what could she do?

The miniature adrenaline particles drifted far from her body, so far that they no longer came under her control, and they grew. And the more they grew, the more Elizabeth coughed. The more she coughed, the more Alice lifted up the airways and toward Elizabeth's mouth.

The adrenaline hit Elizabeth's blood stream, and she awoke in a coughing fit. She hardly noticed Roxton shielding the family, had no idea that Victor stood shouting at her from the doorway, and definitely had no clue that Van Helsing was in the middle of throwing her out of a window.

Elizabeth smashed through the windowpane and hit the ground hard. Her body jerked around, and she spluttered saliva and spittle everywhere. Phlegm burst from her. Elizabeth rose up on her knees and screamed as a balloon of goo birthed itself from her left nostril, expanding the skin around her nose to the size of a golf ball, and deposited itself on the street in front of her. And there stood a sixteen-year-old girl grasping an empty syringe covered in slimy spit.

When the others raced down from the house to check on Alice, they found Elizabeth, quite conscious and relaxed, staring into the sky.

'Alice,' Van Helsing said. 'Are you all right?'

Alice was about to reply but caught a glimpse of what Elizabeth had seen in the sky.

A swarm of police cars arrived on scene, and the officers surrounded Frankenstein's team, yelling at them to put down their weapons.

Roxton looked ready to put up a fight, but Victor insisted they do as requested, and he relented. The uniformed peacekeepers cuffed Roxton and Victor. Alice and Elizabeth continued to stare into the sky.

Eventually, the police and the others noticed something amiss and looked up at the twenty floating pirate ships that poured out of a giant portal.

'What is that?' the officer cuffing Van Helsing's arms said.

'It's Hook,' Victor said. 'She's opened the portal to Neverland.'

'Well, we can't do much in handcuffs,' Roxton said.

Elizabeth stood up, still staring at the ships soaring through the clouds, and police officers attempted to restrain her. She touched the scar on her chest, where her loving husband had forced Peter's heart into her body. 'Pirates,' she said quietly.

Roxton spun to face her. 'Yes, bad men. Bad men come to hurt us all.'

'Bad ... men?' Elizabeth asked.

Victor smiled at her. 'Very bad.'

Elizabeth slammed her fist into her open hand, which caused a clash from metal and bone impacting to rattle through the air. 'We ... fight ... bad men!'

CHAPTER TWELVE

PIRATES

Hook flew down through the thunderous, raining night sky, clutching the portal projector with her arms wrapped around its cylindrical shape.

She landed on top of the National Gallery with a splash as her purple leather boots collided with the damp roof. Morgan waited for her, having picked the perfect place to let the ships come through.

The statue of Lord Nelson would witness the epic arrival of Hook's fleet of pirate ships, all flying through the portal and conquering the entire country.

Hook placed the device down and tilted the lens on top, so it pointed directly upwards.

'Activate the machine, Hook,' Morgan said, flittering around her ear. 'And bring through your entire armada.'

'You know, little fairy,' Hook said. 'I was quite content living in Buckingham Palace. Do I really need to bring my ships?'

'They were about to destroy the entire palace just to be rid of you,' Morgan said, still flittering. 'You need a show of force so great, so unbelievable, that they surrender to you. And you should not accept anything less than complete domination over this entire country. Give them a few years, and they'll worship you. With the technology that you've brought here, you wouldn't have to stop at England. This place has so many countries to take.'

'I would be Queen of the entire world,' she said to herself, smiling, and imagining just what her crown would look like. 'And it all starts tonight, right here, right now.'

Morgan flew away from Hook, ready for her to power up the machine.

Hook looked down at Frankenstein's device and held out her hooked hand. It transformed into its cannon shape and let out a blast of blue electricity.

The portal device powered up and shot a beam of energy up into the sky. Raindrops fizzed and evaporated when they hit the climbing beam of power, which burst apart the clouds and opened its magical doorway. The portal grew to the size of a small village and, inside, lay the bright blue grid. Pink lightning crackled and spat out of the portal's mouth, and the symmetrical grid pattern disappeared into the distance like a glowing road to infinity.

Hook watched as the grid opened up inside the portal and the entrance to Neverland revealed itself. Bright blue sky filled her vision. It looked to be daylight over there—a stark contrast to the dim, wet night London was having.

'I'll keep this side safe,' Morgan said.

Hook flew up into the clouds and entered the portal, passing directly through the centre of the gaping hole in reality. Once on the other side of the mouth, gravity's grasp let her go, and the feeling of flying changed to one of floating.

Though propelled at terrific speed across the grid, she could feel no momentum. She looked back at the doorway, which seemed impossibly small now, and before she could wonder about why the lightning inside the portal was such a bright pink colour, it spat her into the bright, sunny sky of Neverland.

The wind hit her entire body like a warm hug, but from a solid rugby player. Hook stretched out her arms and flew down and toward the ships that lay docked at the island below her.

In just a moment, Hook realised she wasn't gaining any horizontal speed. The only speed that seemed to be increasing was that of the vertical variety.

She hit the cold water of the surrounding ocean and disappeared under the sea just long enough to work out that her powers seemed intrinsically linked to Morgan, and now that a fantastical neon gateway separated them, she seemed to have lost them entirely.

Her thoughts on this matter got interrupted, however, when she realised all her kicking and swimming wasn't getting her anywhere near the surface. Her metal hook-hand and her heavy boots weighed her down. She continued to sink—about to drown.

In a few seconds, she tore her hook through the laces of her boots and ripped them off. Next came her jacket, discarded at a similar pace, but her heavy hook remained grafted to her arm. It would take her a good fifteen seconds to reach the surface, and she figured she had enough air in her lungs to do the job as long as she didn't panic.

Crocodiles, however, had always been a particularly panic-inducing animal for the Hook family, and the sight of three of them making their way towards her through the bright, clear water gave ample cause to bring on a mild panic attack.

Bubbles of precious oxygen escaped from Hook's face in a muffled scream while she thrashed her limbs ferociously.

Hook's head broke through the surface in a little over nine seconds, and her bouncy, red locks of hair now lay flat across her despondent face. The crocodiles seemed happy to pass beneath her still-kicking legs as she made her way towards The Jolly Roger, which bobbed next to the docks.

As she climbed up the side of the ship, she heard her pirates laughing and drinking. The lack of any ships in the sky told her they were at rest and probably had been for the entire time she'd been gone.

Gibbons lay asleep on the deck of the Jolly Roger, hugging a small barrel of ale and snoring like a wildebeest with a nasal problem.

Hook looked around at the other pirates on the deck, and they stopped laughing and fighting with each other and watched as she stepped over to Gibbons, leaving a trail of wet footprints behind her while seawater poured down her legs.

She kicked Gibbons in the side, and he awoke with a start. 'Gibbons. Ready the men. We're going to war.'

He looked up, startled to see her. 'Captain?'

'Yes, Gibbons, it's me. Now, get the men in order at once.'

He struggled to his feet. 'I thought you were dead.'

He had been by her side since the beginning of her revolution and had never let her down yet. A kick in the ribs to wake him was as gentle as she could be and he was surely eternally grateful that he hadn't woken with a limb missing or being eaten by crocodiles.

'Dead? Why on Earth would you think that?' she asked. 'I'm gone for a week or so, and the lot of you turn into playful children. I expect more from my men; and, Gibbons, I can't help but notice that you are still ... not ... readying ... the men!'

'Well ...' he stuttered. 'It's—it's just that ... it's not my job ... anymore.'

'Not your job?' Hook took a step toward him and put a hand on her power sword, which hung from her belt.

At this point, many of the pirates on land had also stopped fighting and drinking, and climbed onto the large ship, intrigued as to what was occurring. They'd been without a war for a week, and any Lost Boys that hadn't been killed were in hiding and hadn't made a peep. The pirates ached for trouble and violence; anything they could cheer at.

Gibbons looked over Hook's shoulder and stepped back.

'I fired 'im as first mate.' Bill Jukes walked out of the Captain's quarters. He stood taller than any other pirate, and tattoos covered his entire body—some rather beautiful, others lewd and offensive. He looked at Hook. Water dripped from her sullen, soaked hair, which clung to her face like a wet slap.

Hook turned to see his smiling face. 'Jukes. I want the men ready for action now,' she said with as much authority as she could muster. 'We're going to London, and we're going to take the entire city.'

'They won't take orders from you anymore, Hook,'

he said, almost spitting out her name. 'You left 'em. Just as victory was won. Someone had to step up to keep this rabble in order.'

Hook pointed her hook at him. 'You stand down or —'

'Or what?' Jukes took a look at all the pirates now swarming the edges of the ship. 'Why don't you fly up and tell everyone why they should follow you.'

The pirates waited. They wanted action. Hook tried using her cannon, but her hook remained a hook. On the brink of taking over England, she wasn't about to let this buffoon stand in her way. She had risen to the top without any powers, and she didn't need any now.

Jukes laughed and turned to his men. 'She's powerless. Lost all her magics! Is that who you want for a Captain? Is it?'

They all cheered for him. Those turncoats. After everything she'd led them to. They were obviously in need of some reminding of just whom they were dealing with.

Hook swung her eyes back to Jukes, who beamed ear to ear. He'd been waiting for this moment, and would always turn on her given the chance. However, he was worth having on her side for his fighting skills. Better to get the first hit in, she thought.

Hook marched towards him with her hook held out. Jukes reached behind and pulled a pistol from his belt. He fired and hit Hook in her shoulder, but the bullet skimmed the surface of her skin. Blood splashed her neck and trickled down her arm. She didn't stop moving, though; she just focussed on getting back through that portal and regaining her powers. It didn't matter what happened here.

Hook slammed her razor-sharp appendage through Jukes' hand, and he dropped the pistol to the deck. Blood spurted from his mangled limb. He raised his left hand and clenched it into a fist, brining it down hard on Hook's face. She grabbed her power sword and yanked her hook towards her body, which brought his body right up to hers. She powered up the sword and thrust it into his middle.

Jukes' eyes grew large when Hook pushed the sword across his stomach, and his guts released onto the wooden deck.

A confused look crept across his face as Hook pulled out the sword and kicked him to the ground. She walked around his body, which still gurgled with life, and looked up at her pirates who had been cheering for this tattooed man but now went quiet. She stabbed her hook under Jukes' jaw and dragged his bleeding carcass over to the plank.

Gibbons shouted, 'Hook, Hook, Hook, Hook.' Before she reached the plank, all the men had joined in.

She dragged the barely-breathing Jukes onto the wooden plank and stepped back over him. He managed to look up at her as she ordered a cannon placed between his legs. 'There's only one captain on this ship.'

Gibbons rushed up to the heavy gun and lit the fuse.

Silence broke out among the men while they waited for the fizzling spark to make its way into the metal of the weapon.

The explosion blew the plank into splinters and did much the same with Bill Jukes' boy bits. Crocodiles swarmed the chunks that landed in the ocean. Gibbons cheered at the bloodthirsty end to such a vile man.

The rest of the pirates cheered too, and Hook turned to talk to them. 'My glorious pirates. For the last week, I have been in London, living there as a Queen. The people of England are no match for our might, and we have an opportunity to take the entire country for ourselves. We'll be rich. Powerful. And we'll be gone from this ridiculous world of flying children and magical fairies.

'No longer will our lives be contained in this colourful world. No longer will we be subject to the whim of winged imps. I say we should strive for something more. Something adult.'

Hook pointed up at the swirling portal in the sky and its bright blue grid structure, and the pirates cheered for her. 'Through that gateway lies our future and war so awesome you'll have to cut your hand off just to believe you're really there. The people of England are weak. Ready to be taken down. We've taken

Neverland—I think it's time we took back our world. What do you say, my pirates?'

Almost deafening cheers erupted. Amidst the excitement and jubilation, Hook gave the order to ready the entire armada.

CHAPTER THIRTEEN

BAD GUYS

Wrapped in a large trench coat, five sizes too big for her, Tinker Bell and Wendy, still wearing her rather elegant dress with a duffel coat around her, marched into the police station. The reception being empty hampered their concerted effort to barge in and demand their friends' release.

Wendy leaned over the desk and tried to look back into the station. She couldn't see or hear anyone. 'I suppose they're all out dealing with the pirate ships.'

Tink wrestled with her giant coat, which hid her other-worldly armour beneath. Obviously, she wasn't too used to normal clothes. If Wendy spent most of her life being four inches tall, she'd probably wear whatever the hell she wanted too.

'Dealing with them?' Tink said. 'These people are not able to deal with Hook and her pirates. She'll slaughter them all; have they not learnt that?'

'We'll explain it. They'll have to let them out.'

'I'm sure we don't need Victor, though,' Tink said with a deep scowl. 'The man can't even fight, and he just seems to make everything worse. I think he's just where he deserves to be.'

Wendy didn't want to agree with her friend, but she found she also couldn't disagree with her. Victor's actions had left her feeling so alone. This man she trusted had taken that which meant the most to her, and pulled it to pieces for his gain without any regard for what it may do to her. She found herself in an impossible position—she truly felt Victor was the only one who could now send the fleet of pirate ships from a parallel dimension back to where they originated.

The radio had reported that the ships had spread out over London, hovering above the entire city and covering every inch of it. The police had been called out in force, and the people had been told to stay indoors. Anyone sleeping at this time of night would have been woken by the immense panic from those awake.

People in their cars filled the streets, trying to flee the city. Others simply wanted to watch the impossible ships float in the air the way that ships are not usually known to do. Wendy and Tink had to contend with the panic and chaos outside just to get to the police station. Now they had made it inside, it felt more than a little frustrating that no one remained around to help them.

Tink began taking her coat off. 'Well, if no one's guarding them, let's just take them out.'

'No.' Wendy put out a hand to stop her. 'We can't just break them out of jail.'

'Of course I can,' Tink said. She pulled back her coat to reveal her enormous hand cannon in her leg holster. 'I can blast any locks.'

'That's not what I meant. We can't get them in any more trouble.'

'We can't exactly make it worse.'

'But ... we're not the bad guys.'

'Can I help you, ladies?' a police officer asked, who had just entered the station along with a few of his colleagues and a gentleman in a rather exquisite grey suit and tie.

Tink stomped her little feet up to the officer and jabbed her finger into his chest. 'I want my friends out of this building at once.'

The other officers showed the gentleman in the suit to the back of the station. The man looked over at the two of them as Tink continued her tirade of abuse against the confused officer. The man's gaze lingered on Tinker Bell as he disappeared through a door, surrounded by the police officers.

Victor sat in his cell while Roxton stood at the bars, gripping them tightly.

'Look here,' Roxton said, putting on his poshest, most respect-demanding accent. 'My name is Lord John Roxton. I demand to see whoever is in charge of this facility.'

No one answered.

Van Helsing and Alice looked across from their cell opposite. Alice had been stripped of her miniaturization suit and put in plain overalls. They had been talking for a while now, apologising to one another and pouring out their feelings. Roxton had listened to them for as long as he could stand and his loud interruption came as something of a relief for both him and Victor.

As far as Roxton could tell, Van Helsing felt sorry that she had held Alice back, and Alice was sorry for running off to save lives. He couldn't comprehend either of them and, though occasionally over the past twenty minutes they had looked over to him for acknowledgment of their apologies, he had simply smiled back at them and wished they would shut the hell up and just get on with life. Life, which at this point, meant figuring out how to get out of this damn police station.

He had asked Van Helsing if she could perform some kind of incantation to open the locks magically, but he had been told, along with a stern look, that what magics she knew, didn't work like that. He now believed that her famous knowledge of the dark arts had all been added to her stories to sell newspapers. Much like the way he himself would embellish his stories a little in his books to add a sense of danger and excitement to his expeditions.

On his last trip to that strange island in the Pacific, he had failed to come back with any evidence of the living dinosaurs he found there. So his book describing the perilous journey that he and Professor Challenger took had contained some minor poetic licence. It brought him fame and money, of course, but soon that waned.

The Amulet of Cthulhu would have brought some accolades, and already he thought about how to structure the book, telling of its capture. But Frankenstein's telegram couldn't have come sooner. Not only was he now able to tell the world about his adventures with flying pirate ladies and magical fairies, but also of Frankenstein himself and his obsession with reanimating his dead wife.

Elizabeth had evaded police capture and currently roamed the streets of London looking for pirates to smash. The book would be pointless, of course, if he weren't the one delivering the fatal blow to Hook, or capturing Elizabeth. He must be the hero, and that would prove rather difficult—no, impossible—whilst stuck inside this damn police station. 'Sergeant,' he yelled again. 'Is anyone out there?'

Two officers walked in, along with the suited gentleman.

'Pipe down, Mr Roxton,' one of them said. 'There's a good chap.'

'It's Lord Roxton, I'll have you know. I have done nothing other than save lives tonight, and I demand that I be set free. This is utterly ridiculous.'

The suited man stepped forward and looked past Roxton and over to Victor, who sat sheepishly on the bed at the back of the cell. Roxton recognised an educated man when he saw one. Probably Eton, he guessed. Always thought they were smarter than everyone around them, Etonians.

'Nice suit,' Roxton said. 'John Phillips. London. I have two myself.'

'Victor Frankenstein?' the man said, ignoring Roxton's mutterings. Victor looked up. 'My name is Mycroft Holmes. I gather you are the one who ... created this device, which has wrought such ... havoc on our city?'

Frankenstein stood and walked over to the bars. 'I suppose so,' he said.

'How does the machine work?' Mycroft asked. 'It opens a hole in space to somewhere else?'

'I doubt you'd be able to comprehend it, Mr Holmes,' Victor said. 'However, I guess you'd like to know how to use it to get rid of those pirate ships in the sky?'

'Oh, I would very much like that,' Mycroft said. 'But you're not going to tell me, are you? Why not?'

'My team has already defeated this woman. Let us go and stop her ourselves.'

'No.' Mycroft turned around and looked at the women in the other cell. 'I think you've caused enough damage to this city already. Tower Bridge? Buckingham Palace? Not to mention the police officers torn apart by your... reanimated wife?'

He took a moment and breathed in heavily. 'I have a suggestion. You'll come with me and tell us how to use this device of yours to send these ships back, and I'll make sure you spend a long time in jail.'

'That doesn't sound like much of an offer, Mr Holmes.'

Mycroft clarified, 'Instead of the death penalty.'

Van Helsing approached the bars of her cell. 'Victor, tell them how to use the device. I don't think we're going anywhere.'

'It'll take too long to explain,' Victor said. 'Just let us go, and we'll get to it and send them back.'

'Doctor Frankenstein, this team of yours is a blunt instrument. You're amateurs, playing a dangerous game in a world full of innocent people. Lives have been lost. You do understand that, don't you? Innocent lives have been taken, and it's all your fault. Just leave the fighting to the professionals.'

'Fine, I'll tell you what to do.'

Mycroft waved the officers over. 'Bring him out.' He looked pleased with himself.

'Where are we going?' The policemen opened the cage and led him out, shutting the door back on Roxton.

'Mission control,' Mycroft said. 'We have an aerial attack on the ships about to commence.'

The officers had been explaining the charges brought against Victor and the others to Wendy and Tink for a while now and had even threatened to throw them inside a cell too. They wouldn't even allow Wendy and Tink to see their friends, and asked them politely to leave the station.

The two women stood on the street in front of the building, unsure what to do. Several of Hook's pirate ships floated in the sky.

'Then I do it alone,' Tink said. 'I'll work out how to beat her.'

'And we just hope the armed forces here can take down an entire fleet of magical flying pirate ships?' Wendy asked.

'Or we break out the others, and we take her down once and for all,' Tink said.

'I think maybe we should leave this to the professionals,' Wendy said. 'None of us are soldiers here. Not even you.'

'That was true many years ago,' Tink said with a

mean, aggressive look on her face. 'But I can't remember not being at war.'

The sound of fighter planes filled the heavens and cut their conversation short. Wendy and Tink watched as the squadron of Spitfires tore across the night sky and launched an attack on the nearest ship. Before long, Wendy could see that they were hopelessly outgunned. The pirate ships seemed near bullet proof, and the cannons poking out of their hulls turned state of the art single-seat fighter aircraft into junk scraps of torn and twisted metal and splashes of evaporated body parts and blood.

Wendy gulped, thinking of the poor pilots, who were dying by the second. 'Okay ... let's go storm the police station and break them out of jail.'

Tink looked up at the horror on display in the sky and smiled at Wendy. Then she ripped open her trench coat and cracked her neck. 'Okay. Let's go be bad guys.'

RICK BUSH

CHAPTER FOURTEEN

BATTLE IN THE SKIES

Hook stood on the deck of the Jolly Roger next to Gibbons, who ordered the crew to head towards Buckingham Palace. It still amused her to see the men pulling ropes and turning cogs to make the ship turn through the air and rise or fall. The knowledge of the fairies had made their ships unbeatable death dealers, and the Jolly Roger had upgraded plasma cannons.

The plan was a simple one: spread the armada across the entire city of London and wait for the inevitable attack. After they destroyed the military's planes, they would land the ships and storm Number Ten Downing Street. Surrender would be accepted, and the country would have a new leader.

As Hook's ship made its way into position, she couldn't help but imagine the world after that night.

Her first orders as leader of England would be purely selfish, of course. A magnificent home for herself, and homes for all her men. She would consult with the current governing body and shape a new government with herself as head. Naturally, anyone disagreeing with her would be killed. Perhaps the people of England would enjoy that. Maybe she'd make it public? Rules never went down too well in Neverland, and her men would get restless quickly if she told them to settle down and have families.

These were men of action; men of fighting and looting. She would have to give them free rein over the entire country. Keeping the people happy with this would take some doing, however. Perhaps Hook could send all the prisoners in the country to live somewhere and just have that as a place where her men could go to pillage and destroy whenever they felt the need. They were options—thoughts and musings. Things she could work out the finer details of at a later date. Right now, her mind had to be on the battle.

The ship steadied to a halt over the top of Buckingham Palace, and Hook looked over the side at the city below. How many people still slept? They would soon wake. Hook turned back to Gibbons.

'Warm up the plasma cannons,' she said with joy. 'If

they want to destroy this palace so badly, I say we give them a hand.'

Gibbons barked out the order, and the men took their positions, readying the cannons.

Hook lifted her arm and watched it transform into its weapon form. Her powers had come back, just as she had suspected they would. She felt curious as to why Morgan had not informed her of the fate of her powers were they to be split up like that. She'd get her answers soon enough.

Morgan flew up over the side of the ship carrying the portal device, which had been deactivated once all the ships had passed through. She hovered above Hook's shoulder. 'You took longer than I thought,' Morgan said. 'The authorities have been investigating the portal. I think they plan to attack.'

'The men needed sobering up, and that wasn't easy without my powers, little fairy.'

'You lost your powers when you went through the portal?' Morgan widened her eyes. 'Interesting.'

Hook grabbed the fairy out of the sky and held her by her legs. 'Yes, very interesting, Morgan. I was nearly eaten alive by crocodiles. Remember our bargain, dark sprite. You get me control of this country, and you can have Neverland.'

Morgan struggled out of Hook's grip and flew out of her reach. 'I'll make sure of it. I'm not going anywhere until Tinker Bell is dead.'

Both of them turned to look out over the horizon when the sound of engines cut through the sky, heading towards them.

———

Flying Officer James Bigsworth, call sign 'Biggs', brought his Spitfire into formation behind the squadron. The plane was new to him, just as it was to the rest of the pilots, but he'd put his brief training to good use. He kept the stick steady and listened to the orders from Squadron Leader Pennington over the radio.

'Okay, boys,' Pennington said with a heap of static. 'We're all wrapping our heads around the fact we have flying ships in the sky, but our mission isn't to debate physics. It's to bring them down.'

The giant hole in the sky had now disappeared, leaving the flying pirate ships hanging above the city of London, which just now came into sight. Their orders were simple: Take down the ships at all costs.

As the city came into view, so did the pirate ships. Their sails flapped in the heavy winds, and strange glowing lights under the hull seemed to be what kept them afloat in the sky. Biggs had no clue how the technology worked, but he bet that was where the power came from.

The squadron flew underneath the first ship, and cannons rang out behind them. A couple of their

Spitfires received hits and headed to the ground with smoky trails.

'Attack formation delta,' Pennington said over the radio. 'Strafe the deck.'

Biggs pulled up on the stick and circled around, and the other craft followed. The planes in front of him rose above the ship and made their descent toward the flying pirates.

The bullets from his squadron's 20mm cannons hit the deck. The pirates on board flinched but then laughed when the bullets bounced off some invisible force field. The Spitfires passed over the ship, and another folly of cannon fire took out more planes.

'Biggs,' Pennington said over the radio. 'Start your descent with me. Take out the mast.'

Biggs yelled over the static, back into his radio, 'Our guns have no effect, this is suicide.'

'Get on my wing and take the shot,' Pennington yelled back.

Biggs manoeuvred his plane just behind the Squadron Leader, and they both headed for the ship, firing their guns.

The pirates ahead of them readied the cannons to fire, just waiting for them to make their pass. Biggs couldn't believe he was following this damn order.

With a brief streak of colourful light, Pennington's Spitfire broke in two with a hit from the right. Biggs glanced out of the cockpit but saw nothing. Pennington's plane crashed into the invisible barrier that surrounded the ship, and Biggs did a barrel roll and dived under the ship. That's when he saw it: The bright purple bullet that had taken down Pennington. The tiny, purple fairy that had been talked about for the past week. The one with Hook who took control of Buckingham Palace.

He fired his guns, and must have gotten her attention, as the purple stream of energy fired from her hands passed by his cockpit, illuminating everything inside for a brief moment. Biggs wasn't prepared to wait and see what would happen if it hit his plane, and so fired back just as Morgan propelled herself away and up into the sky, firing at the remaining planes in the squadron.

How were the other attacks going with the other ships? Most likely, they were having just as much luck as he.

A voice fizzed through static from his radio. 'Biggs, this is Talbot, come in.'

'Talbot, how many are left?'

'You, me, and Perry, it would seem. Let's get back to our attack position and strafe the deck one more time.'

'That's crazy, Talbot; it doesn't work. I think we should try hitting them from underneath.'

'I'm in charge now, Biggs,' Talbot said. 'Get back in formation.'

Biggs felt certain he would die tonight. Too much chaos reigned. Pirate ships. Fairies. Cannons. The

Squadron Leader had died, and Talbot had taken control. Biggs grabbed his stick and ignored his orders. He broke off combat with Morgan and spun upside down to perform a long dive back toward the ground.

'Biggs,' Talbot yelled. 'Get back here.' Talbot flew along with Perry, about to start their descent toward the ship, and be blasted into cannon fodder.

Biggs skimmed his plane across the streets of London below and pulled up sharply on the stick. His Spitfire roared against the G-forces as he rose into the sky until his nose pointed straight up. He kept pulling on the stick until the city lay above him, and in front of him loomed the bottom of the ship.

Pennington's strafe attack was a good idea, but he wasn't thinking three-dimensionally. These ships hovered in the air with all their cannons on the top. A barrage of 20mm cannon fire from his Spitfire would be put to better use coming from underneath where all the bright lights and futuristic tech seemed to be placed.

There was a chance his bullets would simply bounce off the force field yet again, but at least the pirates couldn't aim their cannons at him.

As Biggs closed in on the ship, Talbot and Perry made their descent, firing. Biggs pulled the trigger and fired his guns.

Splinters. An array of splinters exploded from the bottom of the ship as every bullet hit its mark. The bright, glowing lights from the bottom smashed, destroyed. And, as Biggs passed the ship, he looked back to see the ship tip to its side. Talbot and Perry passed over the ship safely, with no cannon fire, and all three of them banked around to witness the entire ship capsize in mid-air. Pirates fell to their deaths from the now-upside-down ship, which continued to rotate in the air as it headed at speed across the city sky, towards central London. Other pirates held onto the rigging or the long ropes, which protruded from the hull.

Biggs fired at the side of the ship and saw that the force field had gone down. A strafe across the deck may get rid of the rest of the pirates.

'Was that you, Biggs?' Talbot asked.

'Afraid so, Sir,' Biggs said. 'Ready for that attack formation now.'

The ship righted itself, and the pirates on board made use of the brief moment of horizontal to man the cannons.

The three Spitfires tore through the sky and ripped the deck apart, taking out six men and several cannons. One single cannon fired, however, and the cricket-ball-sized lump of metal shot towards Biggs' propeller and impacted right in his engine block.

Biggs wrestled with the stick but lost control. His plane slammed into the wooden surface of the pirate ship and came to a halt at the bow. He tried his radio, to call for help, but it had gone dead, and he would be too if he didn't move. He pulled off his air supply and un-holstered his service revolver.

The cockpit glass slid back easily, and Biggs jumped out of the plane and faced three pirates, all advancing on him holding swords. He aimed his gun but got propelled toward the side of the ship when it kept turning. The pirates joined him, slamming against the wood next to him. His gun slipped from his hand and fell to the deck below. One pirate grabbed him, still trying to attack with no care for his life. He pulled at Biggs, trying to peel him off the side and throw him over before the entire ship once more hung upside down.

Biggs punched him in the face and tried reaching for his gun while the other two pirates made their way toward him. The pirate took the punch well, and the mighty blow he returned to Biggs knocked the wind out of him. The pirates now lay on the side of the ship and could fall to their deaths at any moment. Biggs needed that gun.

The ship toppled over once more. The gun slipped into the sky and fell to Earth. Biggs and the pirate followed. The pirate screamed at him, brandishing a blade, as the ship above them grew smaller and smaller and they fell through the sky.

At that precise moment, Biggs wished he could defy gravity much like the fairy he had been dogfighting. He managed to turn his body, and the ground hurtled toward him. The pirate caught up with him, ready to slit his throat. Biggs then saw his weapon, right there in front of him, also falling to Earth.

He reached out and grabbed the gun just as the pirate grabbed his foot, ready to shove the blade into Biggs' chest. Biggs spun around and fired into the pirate's face, and he hung there above him, lifeless, as Biggs continued to head to his inevitable death.

However, when Biggs hit the ground, the soft impact surprised him. The only thing more surprising than the impact was the warmth that came from whatever he'd hit. Then he noticed the hugging. Two arms held around his body, holding on to him, and then he saw a face. A beautiful angelic face with green wings buzzing behind it.

The fairy brought Biggs to the ground, and he dropped to his knees, breathing heavily.

'Thank you,' he said when he'd recovered somewhat. Then he looked up at the people stood before him. 'Who are you?'

'My name's Tinker Bell,' the fairy said.

Victor Frankenstein walked up to Biggs. 'I suggest you take a back seat to this fight.' He helped Biggs up. 'We've got this covered.'

CHAPTER FIFTEEN

BREAKOUT

Tinker Bell pulled out her large side arm as she and Wendy walked back toward the police station. She rarely used it, preferring to rely on the energy blasts from her hands instead. They gave her more control and precision, whereas the plasma blasts from her gun were so destructive, and even Tink would have to guess what the outcome would be. 'Let's make an entrance,' she said. She fired her gun at the front doors and they exploded in a shattering of wood and glass, and smoke and fire engulfed the reception area.

Tink and Wendy stepped inside. Police officers led Victor out of the cell area.

Another benefit of the plasma gun over her energy blasts was the fact that she could hold the gun at someone's head and get them to do anything she wanted. When she levelled her fist at someone's face, it didn't quite have the desired effect.

'Let him go, right now,' Tink said with a stern voice.

'This is going to get you in a lot of trouble, young lady,' Mycroft said. He pulled out a revolver from his jacket and pointed it at her head. 'Quite a display of destruction. However ... if you want to take Doctor Frankenstein with you, I think you've chosen the wrong weapon to threaten me with. Fire that gun and you'll surely kill both of us. Now back off. I have a country to save.'

A look from Wendy made Victor step forward and plead with Tink to stand down.

'These people know what's best, Tinker Bell,' Victor said. 'The Air Force is attacking as we speak. When they retrieve the portal device, they'll need me to send the ships back.'

'They have no chance without the rest of us,' Tink said. 'How many more people are you going to let die, Doctor?'

Frankenstein had to make a choice. A choice between doing the right thing and being utterly reckless. So far, being reckless had caused him and his friends a lot of pain and suffering, so it surprised him when he elbowed Mycroft in the face, snatched the gun out of his hand, and pointed the weapon at the officers.

'Sorry, Mr Holmes,' Victor said. 'But Tinker Bell's right. We have a better chance of stopping this invasion ourselves.'

Victor led Roxton, Van Helsing, and Alice out of the station as Wendy pulled up in Victor's car.

'We borrowed the car,' she said. 'Also brought a few bits from the lab.'

Victor trained his gun on the officers while the three former prisoners climbed into the car.

Tink looked over at a police car pulling up behind them. 'Looks like we have some company.'

Victor got into the passenger side of his car. 'Slow them down.'

'I'll meet you in central,' she said and blasted an energy beam from her hand to just in front of the police car, which sent an explosion of concrete spraying over the windscreen.

Wendy slammed her foot down on the accelerator and sped off while the police officers inside the car ducked beneath the dashboard.

A squadron of planes headed for the ships in the air, and Tinker Bell flew up to join the fight.

Wendy darted the car through the dark streets of London while Alice pulled on her miniaturisation suit in the back, elbowing both Roxton and Van Helsing, who sat either side of her, impatient.

'Must you do that right this second?' Van Helsing said.

'Hey, you're all ready for action. Victor has that metal glove thing. I wanna be ready.' She zipped up the front

The sound of sirens caught up with them and bright blue flashing lights filled the rear window.

'I don't think these boys are giving up,' Roxton said.

'As long as they're not slowing us down,' Victor said, looking in the wing mirror. 'We'll all be fighting pirates sooner or later.'

The entire wing mirror smashed into pieces when a bullet skimmed the car. The police had opened fire.

Alice scowled as everyone hunched down in their seats. 'What the hell is their problem?'

Wendy tried to concentrate on the road. 'We did just destroy a police station and break you guys out. What are we supposed to say? Don't shoot, we're the good guys?'

'Let's just lose them,' Victor said. 'Turn down here.'

Wendy took the next right and slammed her foot hard on the accelerator.

Tink flew up through the squadron of fighter planes and circled the pirate ship above. Other squadrons all over London spewed useless bullets and explosions in the skies, leaving tiny figures dangling from parachutes and inviting a folly of cannon fire.

This wasn't the first time she'd been up against a pirate ship alone, and taking on the entire fleet would be useless. The fighter planes seemed to be outgunned by the extra-dimensional ships. It wasn't the fault of the pilots; they just had no idea where to attack. If she could somehow get them to follow her lead.

The ship's shields were up, but Tink knew exactly how to bypass them. The warrior fairy shrunk down to her fairy size and darted into the ship through a cannon port. Quickly, she regrew to size, startling the pirates inside, and then made her way through the galley, lighting every man up with blasts of energy.

An idea had formed in her mind and it meant taking out every crew member on board without destroying the shield generator. They would never win in a fight against The Jolly Roger without a pirate ship of their own, and Tinker Bell planned to wade her way through body after body until the entire vessel was hers.

Wendy dropped down a gear and screeched round another corner, only to find the entire road blocked with empty cars. People stood beside their vehicles, watching the crazy battles in the sky.

The car skidded to a halt and Wendy slammed the

car into reverse and backed her way out of the street. The police car stopped at the turning, and an officer stepped out, brandishing his weapon. Victor pushed Wendy's head down just as the entire back window burst into thousands of pieces, showering everyone in glass.

Wendy screamed and pushed harder on the accelerator, speeding past the police, forcing the gun-toting officer to leap onto his bonnet to avoid becoming a smear on their tyres.

Wendy looked up and spun the wheel as hard as she could, put the vehicle in first gear, and then pushed down hard on the pedal.

Roxton looked through the non-existent rear window. The police hurried back into their car.

'They're still coming,' he said. Then he turned to Van Helsing. 'What about one of those spells of yours? You love writing about them; how about you actually use one.'

Van Helsing picked shards of glass out of her hair. 'They're a last resort.'

'I think we're a little out of options here.'

Van Helsing reached into her coat and pulled out a small pouch of dried leaves.

'A luck spell?' Alice said.

'I think it's what we need.' Van Helsing poured the leaves into her hand and crushed them into a fine powder. 'There are consequences, however.'

'What kind of consequences?' Roxton asked.

'The Universe is balance. I give us good luck for a while, and the bad soon fills its place.'

More gunshots rang out behind them.

Roxton ducked once more. 'I'm willing to take the chance. Let's do this.'

'I need a light.'

Roxton brought out his lighter. The vampire hunter held out her hand and told Roxton to light it. As he lit the powder in her palm, Van Helsing blew the contents around the car, which caused a huge flame to engulf the interior of the vehicle.

Victor jerked his body away from the flame, jabbing his metal power glove against the window, and smashing the glass to pieces.

Wendy patted her singed hair. 'What the hell are you doing?'

'Is that it?' Roxton said.

Van Helsing nodded with a glint in her eyes. 'That's it.'

Everyone looked out of the window and watched as the police car drove over the shattered pieces of glass. Then it skidded across the road when the left front tyre exploded into frayed chunks of rubber.

'Luck spell?' Roxton said. 'Luck spell, my perfectly formed arse. Victor smashed the window. That was pure —'

'Luck?' Van Helsing said. 'Were you expecting a

glowing orb to propel the car away? Physics is physics.'

Wendy laughed at the empty road ahead of them, which would lead them directly to central London. Even the traffic lights stayed green.

Tink fused the lock on the door to below decks with her energy blast, which trapped the twenty or so pirates she hadn't killed, and turned her attention to the guy behind her.

Tink deflected his gunfire with a quick force field projection and blasted the pistol out of his hand. She threw the last standing pirate against the deck and pushed her plasma gun into his face. 'Option one, I pull the trigger and blow your face off. Option two, you tell me Hook's plan, I let you jump over the side, and you take your chances.'

The pirate, Starkey, wasn't a huge fan of these options but opted to go for number two. Before he made the decision, his brain came up with at least three scenarios in which jumping over the side could end with him living.

Scenario one: Grab onto one of the rappelling ropes on his way down and hang there until help arrived.

Scenario two: Land in a body of water. A lake, pond, or outdoor swimming pool.

Scenario three: Suddenly learn to fly. He'd seen fairies and children do it. Even Hook could do it. Surely some of Tinker Bell's fairy dust must have fallen onto him. All he'd need was a happy thought.

'Option two,' he yelled. 'Option two. Hook's planning to destroy Buckingham Palace and demand the entire country's surrender.'

'That's it?' Tink asked.

'That's it. I swear,' Starkey said, breaking into a sweat.

Tink stepped back, still training the gun at the pirate. She motioned to the side of the ship. 'Off you pop.'

Starkey gulped, pushed his hair back over his small ears, and ran to the edge, then hurled himself over.

Tink grabbed the huge wheel of the ship and piloted it toward the centre of London. The fighter planes around her had seen her heroics and stopped firing. Tink cheered them on as they made their way to another pirate ship.

Tink needed a crew to work the cannons and pilot the ship properly; unfortunately, the ones trapped aboard had broken through the door and now made their way across the deck toward her.

The warrior fairy took the ship into a dive and held on tight while the ship plummeted out of the sky. The pirates rolled around the deck, falling over each other as Tink righted the ship. She'd taken it low, and they smashed through trees and foliage. The war-torn fairy lost her grip and fell to the deck, where she slid along to the stern and into the clutches of the pirates.

'Hello, pretty,' one said and grabbed her shoulder armour. She punched him in the face, knocking him backwards and herself to the ground again, and then the ship came to a halt at last with an enormous splash in St. James' Park Lake.

The rest of the pirates grabbed for her, throwing punches. Tink activated her wings, sending her attackers reeling, and flew from the ship, delivering a quick energy blast to the pirates, ensuring they would follow her.

The pirates dived off the side of the ship and made their way to the bank. Tink landed before them and readied herself for battle, reaching for her plasma gun.

Her holster, however, hung empty.

The soaking-wet pirates climbed out of the lake. The one in front held her weapon. This fight wasn't going as planned.

Her priority was to dodge the onslaught of plasma fire from her weapon, which meant moving as fast as she could while keeping an eye on her attacker and where he had the gun aimed. It gave her no time to return fire, and she'd either be hit soon or be forced to flee.

The pirates kept firing, missing the little fairy with every shot, but a lucky impact on a nearby tree sent the entire wooden giant, branches and all, down on top of

Tinker Bell.

The pirates cheered and walked up to the trapped fairy, who struggled to move. The man with the gun pointed it at Tink, who activated her wings in an effort to fly away. The pirates laughed.

'Stand back, boys,' the man with the gun said. 'This pistol makes a lot of mess.'

The impact of a half-metal woman landing in front of the pirate rocked the entire ground and nearly shook him off his feet.

Elizabeth stood up, and the sound of her metal servos and pneumatic systems unnerved the pirates before her. 'Dark and sinister pirates.' She backhanded the man in front of her, sending him flying off his feet and landing back near the lake. The plasma gun flew from his hand and disappeared with a plop below the surface of the water.

Elizabeth brought her fists up and swung them at the ground with all her might. The earth shook, and the pirates stumbled back.

Then she turned to the fallen tree and grabbed it with both hands. With a heave, she lifted it off Tinker Bell with ease. As soon as the fairy got free, she had to duck because Elizabeth swung the trunk around and threw it at the pirates, who lost a lot of teeth, skin, blood, and pride.

Tink stood, unsure of Elizabeth's intentions toward her. As if in answer, the tall cyborg woman turned to her, smiled, and said, 'We fight ... pirates.'

Victor sat in the passenger seat while Wendy drove the car past Westminster Abbey and came to an abrupt halt. Many pirates ran around, attacking police and civilians alike.

In front of the car, Tinker Bell and Elizabeth fought pirates together.

Victor got out of the car, excited to see his wife. She lifted up a pirate and threw him into the air, where Tink then fired at him.

'Elizabeth,' Victor yelled, but before she could turn to see him, everyone's attention turned toward the giant, spiralling pirate ship in the sky, heading their way.

The team watched as a British pilot fell from the deck.

'Tinker Bell,' Victor shouted, pointing at the sky. 'Man overboard.'

Tink activated her wings and flew up into the sky. The falling man shot a pirate, who had been tumbling through the air behind him. Then the pilot waved his arms about in terror, and Tink scooped him into her arms just before he hit the ground.

Tink landed in front of Victor and his team, and the exhausted airman fell to his knees, breathing heavily.

'Thank you,' he said, looking up at his rescuers.

'Who are you?'

'My name's Tinker Bell,' Tink said.

Victor walked up to the pilot. 'I suggest you take a back seat to this fight.' He helped him up. 'We've got this covered.'

'I've still got bullets in my gun,' Biggs said. 'I'd rather put them to some use.'

Victor's league prepared for battle. Roxton pulled out his twin semi-automatics and cracked his neck.

Alice handed Van Helsing a couple of battle axes from the boot of the car, and Wendy passed Victor the German Mauser pistol he kept in his study.

Victor took the gun but held his gaze on Wendy. 'Maybe you should take the car and head back.'

Wendy pulled out Peter's power sword and used it to cut off the bottom of her dress, exposing her legs.

'Doctor,' she said. 'I've had more experience fighting these pirates than any soldier here has.' She tore a piece of fabric from her dress and wrapped it around her head to hold the hair out of her eyes.

'Fair enough.' Victor looked over at Elizabeth, who continued to beat the crap out of pirates, and he realised he wouldn't get to speak with her until this mess got cleaned up. Hook had to be taken down, and each pirate ship destroyed, before Elizabeth and he could be together again.

'Get on board the ship,' Tink said to the others. 'I'll meet you on the deck.'

Victor watched the warrior fairy stroll toward the lake. 'Where are you going?'

'I'm getting my gun back.'

CHAPTER SIXTEEN

#

Starkey the pirate hovered about a hundred feet above the ground, increasingly confused, though still deliriously happy, that he wasn't dead.

The intense rush of adrenaline when he fell from the ship had brought a huge smile to his face, even while he plummeted down toward his would be doom. Then his rate of descent slowed until he hung motionless in the air.

He felt ecstatic, elated, and jubilant. Tears of joy streamed down his face when he flew through the air and controlled his levitation.

This was his moment. He would become the pirate

version of Peter Pan, soaring into battle like a leaf on the wind. No longer would his pirate peers mock him. No longer would he ever have to fear attacks from fairies or flying children. He would be the true saviour of all the pirates.

The bullet whipped through Starkey's head in an instant and his smile dropped. As did his body.

Victor Frankenstein holstered his Mauser pistol and watched from the deck of Tink's reclaimed ship as the pirate hit the ground below with a red spray of blood.

Tinker Bell was at the helm and along with Victor, Van Helsing, and Wendy, they each readied their weapons.

'Get in front of the Palace,' Victor said. 'Looks like Hook's readying to fire.'

Tink increased speed and soared the ship through the air toward Buckingham Palace.

Gibbons kept the Jolly Rodger steady, and the men shouted that they were ready to fire. Tink's ship headed straight for them, and he turned to Hook—busy watching the increasing number of British planes falling from the skies all over the London skyline.

'Captain,' Gibbons said. 'It's Tinker Bell. She's coming up on us.'

Hook and Morgan looked over at the ship heading to the Palace.

'I think we've given them something to think about,' Hook said to Morgan. 'Let's step this up and get some men on the ground, shall we?'

Morgan flew up into the night sky and set off an intense flare of sparkling energy, which burst into the clouds.

The ships all over London saw the signal and descended. The pirates on board threw ropes over the side and rappelled to the streets below.

Hook watched as Tink's ship approached them. 'I want that Palace turned to rubble,' she said. 'Fire at will.'

The enormous energy cannons on The Jolly Rodger powered up and fired a beam of intense white light through the London sky, directly at the Palace.

Tink's ship swerved directly into the path of the energy beam, rocking the vehicle to one side and ripping a giant hole in the side of the hull. Buckingham Palace still stood.

Tink pulled her ship up close to The Jolly Roger just as Hook stepped down to the main deck to address her men.

'Can we fire again yet?' she asked.

'Yes, Captain,' Gibbons said. 'But with that ship this close, we'd take ourselves down with it.'

'Then ready yourselves, men.' Hook pulled out her power sword. 'Looks like we're doing this the old fashioned way.'

A cheer erupted from the men as they pulled out pistols and scimitars.

The streets of central London filled up with pirates as they landed on the ground, jumping from the ropes that hung from the ships, which now hovered at house height.

The people on the streets, who had been watching the battle above them, now ran for their lives as the bloodthirsty crew waved their swords and hacked at whoever got in their way. Hook had ordered them to cause panic and chaos enough to force the country's surrender, which would be topped off with the destruction of Buckingham palace.

Alice grasped her croquet mallet tightly and ran up to three pirates harassing passers by. The one grabbing the old man by his jacket saw her and let the frail gentleman fall to the ground. He pulled out his pistol and fired at Alice, who leapt into the air, shrinking as she did so and avoided the oncoming projectile. She landed softly on the ground at his feet.

The pirate only had a moment to react to her disappearance from sight when she rapidly grew back to size and delivered a devastating uppercut to his jaw.

His two colleagues jumped back in astonishment

when the pirate fell to the ground, and Alice swung the wooden mallet around into their faces with a bone-shattering crunch.

Roxton emptied his guns into a horde of pirates and soon ran out of bullets. He holstered his precious weapons as the rest of the pirates in front of him advanced.

Alice ran over to him. 'Roxton,' she yelled. 'Send me their way.' She jumped into the air, shrinking as she did so and landed gently in Roxton's palm. He cupped his hand and threw her tiny body as hard as he could into the swarm of pirates ahead of him.

Alice grew as she rocketed toward the men and collided with them, knocking them over like pins in a bowling alley.

Roxton picked up a sword from the ground and thanked his parents for sending him to Cambridge. They had the best fencing team in the country, and he had been the best in the school. He fought off multiple attackers, besting them with an array of parries, jabs, and bloodletting swipes.

The ace fighter pilot, Biggs, herded the civilians to safety. He kicked open a shop door and hurried them inside. 'Wait here 'til it's over. You should be safe.' He headed back outside where he found himself surrounded by pirates all wanting a piece of him.

As Biggs beat them off one by one, Elizabeth joined the party, lifted one of the bigger men into the air, and threw him into the shop window.

The frightened people inside screamed when the tall, un-dead woman stepped up to the shattered glass panes. Her heart beat so fast; all her body wanted to do was fight the pirates, but a glimpse of her reflection sat uneasily with her.

She recognised the face looking back at her but it somehow wasn't quite her. As her husband's colleagues continued to push back against the pirates behind her, she looked closer at the glass and touched a cold metal hand to her face. Something wasn't right inside her. The outside didn't seem right either.

The scars.

The paleness of her skin.

Her erratic hair. All different.

But her eyes. Her eyes she recognised. They were hers. Elizabeth Frankenstein's. And with that single thought of her married name, another came to the forefront of her mind. 'Victor.' She looked back over her shoulder, up into the sky.

———

'Looks like the ship's shields have failed,' Tink said. 'Can't survive another blast like that.'

'Then get us closer,' Wendy said, powering up Peter's power sword. 'Just like old times.'

Victor Frankenstein grabbed hold of a rope, which

dangled from the towering masts. He looked over at Wendy, who held Peter's power sword in her hand. She looked deadly serious; a side of her that he hadn't seen before. She had often told him tales of her and Peter's adventures, but they were filled with fun and the battles so light-hearted. Were they lies? Or just sugar-coated memories?

The two ships collided.

'Destroy them,' Hook yelled.

Victor powered up his metallic power-glove and gave an almighty war cry.

Van Helsing and Wendy leapt onto the Jolly Roger and swung their swords into the oncoming fray of burly pirates.

Victor swung over the deck, kicked Gibbons to the ground, and landed next to him. He aimed his power glove at him and blasted a good few thousand vaults into his body. The pirate's body went limp and he fell into a deep sleep, silently soiling himself.

Victor turned and pulled out his Mauser once more and fired at any pirate who charged at him. He had to find the portal device and send them all back to Neverland. All he cared about now was saving this world. Neverland would have to live with the pirates; as it had done for the last few hundred years.

Van Helsing plunged her battle-axe into a the chest of a pirate, sending him to the ground. It wedged in his rib cage and a gentle pull wouldn't release it. A snarling, short-bearded man saw this and headed her way, raising his sword above his head, ready to take hers.

Van Helsing pushed her boot on the dead man's shoulder and pulled ... nothing. Just as she was about to meet the business end of a long piece of steel, Tinker Bell flew in, grabbed the bearded pirate, and flung him over the side. The glowing fairy back-flipped in the air and landed in the middle of the deck just as Van Helsing pulled her axe free.

'That's two you owe me,' the fairy said with a wink. Van Helsing launched her axe toward Tink's head, narrowly missing it, and hit a pirate behind her.

'Let's call it even.' The two of them stood back to back, looking at the relentless pirate hordes. Hook stood at the far end of the ship, with the portal device behind her.

Wendy swung Peter's power sword around, blasting the pirates' swords in two and scorching their bodies when she thrust the glowing beam into them. She backed up to Van Helsing and Tinker Bell as Victor rushed toward them.

'I need to get to the portal device,' Victor said. 'Let's clear a path.'

'You can't send them back,' Tink said. 'We must destroy them here. It's the only way to save both our worlds.'

'I'm sorry,' Victor said. 'I have to think about the thousands of innocent people below us.'

Morgan flew in, grew to full size, and fired her energy beams at them. Victor ducked for cover with the others, and as the smoke and cinders settled.

Tink stood and activated her wings. 'She's mine.' With a gust of wind, she flew up after her.

'It's up to us now,' Victor said. 'If I can get hold of the portal device, I can fix this.'

Wendy slashed her power sword against another Pirate, nodded, and the three of them made their way toward the far end of the ship where Hook stood watching.

Wendy ducked when a pirate lunged for her. 'I hope that luck spell is still working for us.'

Van Helsing buried her axe into the pirate's head. 'I'm sure it ran out a while ago.'

Wendy pushed forward and found herself face to face with Hook, who held her bright purple power sword in her hand. Wendy raised hers.

'Ooh,' Hook said. 'Got a little fight in you at last, have you? I like that.'

'I am going to kill you.' Wendy swung her sword at Hook's face. Hook blocked her attack, raised her other hand, and sent Wendy flying back with a pulse of energy.

Hook turned off her sword. 'You're not worth my time.' She grabbed the portal device and held it in her arms.

Victor ran up to Wendy, and they both watched as

Hook floated over their heads toward the back of the ship. Victor fired his gun at her, but the bullets hit a force field around her and pinged off, leaving a purple ripple of light dancing around her.

Hook landed at the wheel and turned the ship, so it headed directly for Buckingham Palace.

'Activate the cannons,' she yelled. A pirate managed to start the firing sequence of the Jolly Rodger's weapons systems.

'Good man,' Hook said. She aimed her cannon hand at the wheel, blasted it into a thousand wooden splinters, grabbed the portal device once more, and flew up into the sky.

The few remaining pirates stopped fighting and tried to balance themselves when the ship turned and sped toward the palace.

Some took their chances with the descending ropes while others cheered for a heroic death.

Victor ran to the side of the ship as their speed increased.

'Can we take the other ship?'

'No time,' Wendy said. 'Where's Tinker Bell?'

Van Helsing grabbed the two of them. 'Get your heads down.' She shoved them to the floor.

The two ships soared out of the sky, across the courtyard in front of Buckingham Palace, and ploughed into the front wall just as The Jolly Roger fired its cannons into the adjoining ship.

The resulting explosion took out the entire left side of the palace, sending bricks and mortar into the streets around it. The Jolly Roger rocketed across the quadrangle at the centre of the palace and exploded when it hit the main building. The roof burst in a spray of bricks, and the entire structure caved in and collapsed, leaving nothing more than a pile of burning rubble where something glorious had once stood.

RICK BUSH

CHAPTER SEVENTEEN

SURRENDER

Tinker Bell soared through the sky after Morgan. An intense look of frustration sat on her face like a burning rash. She wanted to talk properly with her and get her to end this madness. Tink blamed herself for her sister's breakdown and eventual fall into madness and felt determined to fix it.

Morgan fired blast after blast back at Tink, who swerved all over the sky, dodging them one by one. The evil fairy turned around, flying backwards, and built up as much energy as she could in her hands and threw an almighty energy beam at Tink, which skimmed her shoulder.

Tink cried out in pain and un-holstered her gun. She

flew directly into Morgan, grabbed her throat, and pushed the gun against her head. 'You will stop this. Please, Morgan. Enough is enough.'

Morgan seemed calm. Almost pleased with herself. 'I have rid Neverland of every single pirate. Not even Peter Pan could manage that.'

'You don't get to say his name. You haven't saved Neverland ... you've deformed it.'

Morgan shook her head and smiled a sad little smile. 'Sometimes, to make the world a better place, we have to do something ugly.'

An explosion beneath them grabbed Tink's attention, and Morgan blasted her body away.

Tink tumbled through the sky until her wings righted her. She saw Buckingham Palace fall to pieces, and the two ships her friends had been fighting on become no more than burning embers.

———

Mycroft Holmes lifted the receiver of the red phone in his office and listened. He listened to the tale of the destruction of Buckingham Palace and how Hook and her pirates now marched toward Downing Street, demanding surrender. As Mycroft listened to the words coming from the Prime Minister, he lowered his head. The PM asked if there was any alternative. Anything they could do other than surrender that would save lives. Mycroft apologised; his mind was exquisite and usually enriched with ideas that just seemed to fall from his thoughts, but at the moment when he needed ideas the most, his mind went blank. The Prime Minister gave the order to surrender.

———

Tink flew down to the smouldering remains of the enormous building and landed, cracking the concrete beneath her. She ran up to the rubble and saw her friends, held safely within a shimmering, protective bubble. Van Helsing held a small, glowing rock up and sweated profusely while Victor and Wendy crouched beneath her.

'I can't hold it much longer,' Van Helsing said. 'Protection spell never lasts long ... get this stuff off us.'

Tink pulled out her gun and aimed at the top of the bubble. 'Just keep it up for a few more seconds.' She blasted a hole in the bricks and mortar surrounding them.

Van Helsing dropped to the ground, exhausted. Victor caught her and helped her out of the ruins. Beneath them, lay Gibbons with his soiled trousers. He came to and looked around, confused.

Tink grabbed him and pushed her gun against his head the way she had with Morgan.

'No, please ... please, don't kill me,' Gibbons said.

'Give me one reason I shouldn't.'

Gibbons looked ashamed. 'I know how you can best Miss Hook.'

'I'm listening.'

'When she arrived back in Neverland to fetch us, she didn't have her powers.'

Tink loosened her grip on his collar and pulled her gun away from his head. 'Was Morgan with her?'

'No. She was alone.'

Tink dropped him to the ground and caught up with her teammates.

Wendy looked around as she stood at the gates of Buckingham Palace. 'Do you hear that?'

'I don't hear anything,' Victor said.

'Exactly. No one's fighting. You don't think she's done it?'

'I can't believe that.' Victor turned when Tink approached them.

'I think I have a plan,' Tink said. 'If I can separate Morgan from Hook, she loses her powers.'

'Separate them?' Victor's eyes widened. 'How far?'

'We need to send Morgan back to Neverland.'

Victor stood, contemplating his actions. 'So, we find the portal device, I open a doorway to Neverland while the others fight off Hook and her army of pirates, and you fly Morgan through the grid?'

'Exactly,' Tink said. It sounded impossible.

'We'll need to find the others,' Wendy said.

Van Helsing got to her feet. 'I like this plan. I'm excited to be a part of it. So, where's Hook?'

'If we *have* surrendered,' Victor said. 'There's only one place she'll be.'

Biggs, Roxton, Alice, and Elizabeth stood among the soldiers guarding the home of the Prime Minister. Hook marched along Downing Street with a battery of cheering pirates behind her. She held the Amulet of Cthulhu in her hand, running her thumb over its shiny surface.

She had done it; brought London to its knees. Now all that was left was to make it official.

The armed soldiers stood down at her approach and lowered their weapons. Biggs stood firm and trained his handgun on Hook. 'We can't just let her walk in.'

The soldier next to him placed a hand on his arm, lowering it. 'Put it down, lad. We have our orders.'

'But we could end this right now. One shot and she's dead.'

'Orders are orders. Now, put the gun down.'

But Biggs couldn't follow orders that he didn't agree with. He stepped out, raised his gun, and fired.

The bullet ricocheted off an invisible force field around her. Hook raised her hook hand, transformed it into its cannon mode, and sent a pulse of energy straight through Biggs' chest.

He fell to the ground with a smoking hole where his heart had once been.

The rest of the soldiers dropped their guns as quickly as they could, and Hook had her men gather up their weapons and force them to their knees.

Other pirates held Roxton and Alice and pointed guns at the back of their heads.

Elizabeth gave an almighty roar, lunged out of the crowd, and charged for Hook.

Hook smiled and waved her hand at the cybernetic woman running towards her, and then lifted her off the ground in a bubble of shimmering purple light. Elizabeth rose into the air until she resembled nothing more than a speck in the night sky.

Hook turned her attention back to Number 10 and looked up at the building. 'Prime Minister. I suggest you come outside and surrender in person. Or your city will face a great deal more suffering. Starting with these soldiers out here.' She waited for a response—none came. 'Or should I have my men destroy the Houses Of Parliament? Or perhaps you'd rather a huge crater among the houses of central London?'

The door to Number 10 opened, and the Prime Minister walked out. He smoothed his suit before making his way toward Hook.

She greeted the Prime Minister, 'Mr Baldwin, I presume.'

'What is it you want?' he asked.

'Kneel.' Hook pointed to the ground at her feet. 'And surrender your country ... to me.'

'I'll kneel if it'll save lives.'

'It will. It'll save a great many lives.'

The Prime Minister looked down at the ground and over at the soldiers around him, all watching. 'What I do now, I do for the people of England.' He lowered his body to the ground and, swiftly as he could, pulled a knife from his pocket and stabbed Hook in the stomach. 'England will never surrender!'

Hook stumbled back in surprise. Then she spun him around and held his head to her stomach. Her hook penetrated the Prime Minister's soft flesh at his neck, and she ripped a bloody gash under his chin. Blood poured out of the man's body and spilled out onto the street below. With a push, she flung his pale corpse to the ground and watched the small cut on her stomach heal itself. She pointed to Roxton and Alice. 'Bring them here.'

The pirates marched them out in front of Hook and shoved them down to their knees.

'Your friends are dead,' Hook said. 'Your country is mine. Any last words?'

Lord John Roxton reached into his pocket and pulled out a small silver case. He placed a cigarette from the case in his mouth and looked up at Hook. 'You don't happen to have a light do you?'

CHAPTER EIGHTEEN

THE AMULET

Victor Frankenstein ran up to Downing Street from St. James's Park and sprinted past the twisted and destroyed gates. Alice and Roxton knelt in front of Hook.

'It's Alice,' Van Helsing said. 'I have to do something.'

Victor pulled her back. 'They'll only kill you too.'

'I have to try something.' She pulled out another small pouch of dry leaves.

'Another luck spell?' Wendy asked. 'Didn't you say those things eventually bring bad luck?'

'Which is probably why we're in this mess right now.' Van Helsing crushed the leaves in her palm.

'Trouble is, I don't think we have any choice. How much worse can it get?'

Wendy powered up Peter's sword, ignited the dust in Van Helsing's hand. She blew the embers into the air around them.

They looked over at Hook, who held her cannon hand to Roxton's face.

'I'll give you a light,' Hook said.

Morgan flew down and hovered by Hook's face. 'The country is yours. Now give me the portal device so I can go home.'

Hook turned to face Morgan and pulled her cannon away from Roxton's cigarette, which still hung from his mouth. 'You want to leave already, dark sprite?'

'I said I'd help you take the country. And now it's yours. I must return home.'

'I. Don't. Think. So.' Hook snatched Morgan out of the air and gripped her in an angry fist. 'You think I don't know what would happen if you were to head back to Neverland?' Hook shook her. 'I'd lose my powers, wouldn't I? You'd happily leave me defenceless here while you took control of Neverland. That was your plan all along, wasn't it? To get rid of us pirates?'

'I kept my end of the bargain.'

Hook fed her into her cannon hand, which sealed itself shut. Then she held her metallic hand up to her face. 'Now we'll never be separated, little one.'

Tink flew her way over the crowd of pirates,

distracting them from Van Helsing, and barged through the crowd, swiftly followed by Victor, who electrocuted his way through. Wendy activated her power sword as Tink landed beside Hook, and soon they stood face to face with the vicious pirate.

Hook turned to one of her men, pulled an old six-shot revolver from his belt, and fired at Wendy, who vaporised each bullet with quick swipes of her blade.

Roxton grabbed Alice and got out of the way as Wendy charged at Hook, who raised her cannon hand. Wendy brought the power sword down at her wrist and cut her arm in two.

Hook screamed in pain, and the cannon dropped to the ground with a thunk. Morgan flew out, increased her size, and collided with Tink, who punched her repeatedly in the face. The two fairies propelled each other into the sky and shot upward at lightning speed.

The pirates raised their weapons. The soldiers, still on their knees, did likewise.

Victor turned to the soldiers. 'Let's send them home, boys.' With that, the soldiers stood, and a clash of fists on faces started an immense fight on Downing Street.

Hook powered up her sword and lashed out at Wendy. Roxton and Van Helsing edged closer to her and Hook waved around her stump of a wrist, jettisoning erratic bursts of energy. Alice ducked as the blasts hit the front of Number 10 and took the door clean off its hinges.

No one could get close enough to Hook, but plenty of people would get hurt trying.

Wendy yelled to Van Helsing, 'This is what happens when you use a luck spell.'

Van Helsing leapt out of the way of another blast from Hook. 'Just keep your eyes open. Where's the portal device?'

Victor had seen a pirate holding it behind Hook, and was determined to get past her. 'Roxton, I'm going to need some cover here.'

Roxton nodded and dived to the ground as bullets hit the concrete around him. He picked up two military pistols from some downed soldiers and stood up, firing at Hook.

She blocked each bullet with her force field as Victor ran past her, trying to get to the portal device. With a quick swing of her glowing purple sword, she sent one of Roxton's bullets straight back at him, hitting him in the leg.

He fell to one knee, in pain, and flinched when Hook spun around and buried her sword in his shoulder.

Van Helsing looked up as soon as he screamed, grabbed a sword out of a pirate's hand, and threw it at Hook's face. She caught it by the blade and smiled.

Wendy stood in front of Hook, holding up her sword. 'Fight me fair this time,' she said. 'No powers ... let's see your skill.'

'Silly little girl wants to play games.' Hook crashed

her blade into Wendy's.

Van Helsing ran over to Roxton, who bled all over the road. She threw off her long coat and ripped half her shirt off, exposing her toned stomach. Then she made a tourniquet of the strip of fabric around his thigh. 'How are you doing?'

'Not great. I lost my last cigarette.'

Tink and Morgan grappled with each other, sending beams of powerful energy through the clouds as they punched, kicked, and grabbed.

As they flew higher and higher, they approached Elizabeth, still in her shimmering bubble, pounding on the invisible walls.

The two battling fairies flew straight into her, bursting her bubble with an immense purple shockwave and allowing gravity to take hold of Victor's wife once more.

Elizabeth fell through the sky, and the ground rushed at her. Still directly over Downing Street, she seemed to be headed for a crowd of pirates. Would she survive such a fall? The image of a certain man wouldn't leave her mind. That name again, repeating over and over inside her thoughts: Victor.

It meant something to her, but still she couldn't place it. Only that it seemed important to remember.

With that thought lodged firmly in her head, Elizabeth slammed into the crowd of pirates and, immediately after, the hard concrete. Pirates and soldiers alike toppled over at the impact.

Morgan punched Tinker Bell in the face. The fairy un-holstered her gun. Morgan pushed the barrel away and tried to move it towards Tink.

Tink wouldn't allow her to harm any more people, and with all her might, pushed the gun back toward Morgan.

Morgan's head slammed down hard into Tink's nose, bringing tears to her eyes. It took her a moment to realise that Morgan had pulled the trigger and blasted a hole clean through her chest.

Magical energy fell out of Tink's middle like dust in the wind, and Morgan dropped the gun and flew closer to the stunned Tink.

'In order to make the world a better place ...' Morgan said.

Tink grabbed hold of Morgan's top and gripped with all her might, and finished her sentence, '… We have to do something ugly.' With an almighty burst of strength, Tink pulled Morgan toward the ground at a tremendous rate, leaving a bright green, twinkling stream of energy behind her.

Victor pulled himself up from the ground and looked over at his wife, who lay unmoving in a crater in the street. 'Elizabeth.' He made his way toward her, despite the fact that the pirates behind him were taking the portal projector away.

Hook swatted Wendy away with her stump and watched as it reformed into a fleshy hand. Victor rushed past her, toward his wife. Hook grabbed him and pinned him against the wall.

Held against the brickwork, he glanced up at the sky. An intense streak of green energy plummeted toward him.

Hook deactivated her sword and held Victor around the neck with two hands. 'I must thank you,' she said. 'Without you, all this would never have been possible. Now it's time to die.'

Victor turned to the crater. Elizabeth's arm reached up and pulled her body from the destroyed, smoking tarmac around her. 'Elizabeth,' he said. 'You've got incoming.'

Tink jetted past them and aimed straight for Elizabeth, holding Morgan as high above her as she could.

Elizabeth threw the hardest punch her new body would physically allow. Her metallic fist met Morgan's face like a red-hot metal ball, shot from a cannon, making its way through a jam jar, and made just as

183

much mess.

Morgan's body slumped to the ground, now sporting a mushy paste in place of her head. Tink flipped over in the air and landed, looking at her dead sister solemnly. She held her chest while the sparkling magic poured from her and turned into bright red blood.

Victor noticed Hook's grip lessen around his throat, and he grabbed her wrists, pried her off him, and pushed her away.

Hook looked down at Morgan and over at her pirates, whom the British soldiers and Victor's teammates had overwhelmed. She backed up and activated her power sword.

Tink made her way toward her. 'It's over.'

Wendy and Victor joined Tink, and they all advanced on Hook.

Hook waved her sword around. 'Stay back.' She pulled out the Amulet of Cthulhu and held it up.

Roxton pushed into a sitting position, with his bandaged leg stretched out in front of him.

Hook dropped the Amulet on the ground and held her sword above it. 'You want this world? You can have it.' She plunged the power sword into the Amulet and broke it in two. The ground quaked.

Hook grabbed the portal projector from the arms of one of her dead pirates and ran for her life as the entire street shook and cracked. The Amulet glowed, and smoke poured out of its centre. When the road broke apart and huge chunks of concrete lifted into the air, everyone ran.

Crowds of pirates and soldiers alike poured out of the entrance to Downing Street and backed up toward St. James's Park.

A giant fist punched through the street from under the ground, taking half of Number 10 with it. The fist slammed down into the buildings, and a pair of dark green-winged shoulders burst from the road.

Van Helsing helped Roxton to safety and turned to see the giant creature step out of the ground and stand in all its glory.

The creature's head looked like a pulsating mass of flesh with two glowing green eyes. As it turned, looking at its surroundings, its tentacles slithered around its mouth, dropping down around its chest. It towered over the surrounding buildings and stood over five hundred feet tall. With an unearthly scream of pure insanity, it raised its wings and brought its clawed, webbed fists down onto the buildings around it, decimating them into rubble.

Alice and Wendy joined Van Helsing, Roxton, and Victor. They looked up at the beast alongside Elizabeth.

'What do we do?' Van Helsing asked.

Roxton looked up at her. 'No more luck spells.'

RICK BUSH

CHAPTER NINETEEN

EAT ME

Elizabeth stared at her husband. 'Victor?'

He took her hands. 'Yes, Elizabeth, it's me.'

'I feel odd,' she said.

'I know ... but you're here ... and we're together. That's all that's important now.'

Elizabeth felt physically cold to his touch, but the warmth in her eyes told him everything. She was his for all eternity. She loved him with all her heart.

Victor held his dead wife's hands and looked into her eyes. It was her; alive and fully aware of who she was. They were together again. He had so many questions, so many things to say to her, but all they had time for was this brief moment as the giant tentacled monster tore their city apart.

Roxton broke into the moment. 'It's an ancient deity from the beginning of time called Cthulhu,' he said. 'If he's been trapped in that Amulet all this time, I'd think he's probably a little pissed off.'

'That ancient deity will destroy London,' Victor said. 'How do we stop him?'

They watched the giant creature pound his way through the streets and topple every building in his path.

'You can't,' Roxton said. 'He's a giant god. We're like insects to him. We wouldn't even get his attention.'

Alice grabbed Victor's arm. 'You made my suit shrink,' she said. 'Can't you make it do the opposite?'

'Theoretically, yes.' Victor glanced at Van Helsing. 'But stretching your atoms apart would be highly dangerous. If you expand your size to match this Cthulhu, you could very well explode. And not after a minute, but at any time.'

Cthulhu waded across the river, grabbed hold of Westminster Bridge, wrenched it from its foundations, and lifted it into the air. The monster then threw the bridge across the city, destroying Waterloo train station.

'Thousands of people are dying as we speak,' Alice said. 'Make it work, and I can try and stop him.'

Van Helsing interrupted her. 'Alice, this is crazy. That thing will tear you apart.'

'Let me do this,' Alice said. Her voice was like steel and her eyes burned with determination. 'I can at least try and keep him in one place while you find the portal device.'

'Of course.' Victor nodded. 'We'll open a portal to deep space and send him through.' He fiddled with the controls of Alice's wired overalls.

Van Helsing looked around her. 'That means finding Hook. Where's Wendy?'

Hook had run onto Westminster Bridge just as Cthulhu had grabbed hold of it. When she opened her eyes, she saw that the middle of the bridge was no longer in place, and if she had been twenty feet further along, she'd have been thrown into the river.

The portal device still lay beside her, and she knelt down and tried to activate the mechanism. Without any more power, she hoped there would still be enough juice in it to open a small portal to Neverland so that she could retreat.

While Hook focused the lens on top of the device, she became aware she was not alone on the short nub of bridge. Behind her stood Wendy with her glowing power sword.

'You don't get to leave, Hook,' Wendy said. 'Not from this.'

Hook unfastened her sword hilt from her belt and activated the purple blade.

'You're right,' she said. 'The end is important in all things.'

Wendy took a step forward. 'And this ends tonight.'

Their swords clashed together.

Victor twisted two tiny wires together and turned Alice around. 'All right, that should do it.'

Alice looked over at Van Helsing, knowing she disapproved, but this was the only choice; their only chance.

Van Helsing took a step closer and gave a small, proud smile. 'Can you do this?'

'I'll do all I can,' Alice said.

'Then go kick its arse.'

Alice smiled and told everyone to back away from her. She balled her hands into fists, closed her eyes, and concentrated hard. Then she imagined herself swelling, growing, expanding, and soon she felt light headed.

Upon opening her eyes, she lost her balance and fell forward onto her hands. She had reached fifty feet tall and continued to grow. Alice stood up once more and grew another fifty feet in a matter of seconds.

She took in a large breath of air and nearly passed out from the amount of oxygen in her lungs. Alice could now see the river over the roofs of the buildings in front of her and the enormous god creature still loomed a lot taller than her.

Wary, she made her way to the river, stepping around vehicles and buildings, and stood on the bank, and (painfully) tried to increase her size some more to match the giant in front of her. 'Oi, tentacle face!' she yelled. 'Come step on someone your own size.'

Cthulhu turned around slowly and looked Alice dead in the eyes. A tilt of his head showed some semblance of curiosity. He stepped back towards the river until he stood on the opposite side.

Beneath and to the right of Alice, stood Wendy and Hook, still lighting up the darkness with their clashing of power swords.

Victor, Elizabeth, and Van Helsing ran onto the south bank and came to an abrupt halt when they witnessed the two five hundred feet tall giants step into the river and grapple with each other while Wendy and Hook battled beneath them.

'Look,' Victor said. 'It's Wendy and Hook.'

'I can help her.' Elizabeth made her way over to what remained of Westminster Bridge.

'Wait.' Victor held her back. 'It's personal. She has to do this alone.'

'Why?' Elizabeth said.

'Yeah, why?' Van Helsing asked.

'Good point,' Victor said. 'Let's go help.'

The three of them ran over to the duelling duo as Alice brought her knee up into Cthulhu's groin.

He didn't even flinch, and Alice had to presume that either he didn't feel pain at all or she had miscalculated where his sexual organs were placed.

Cthulhu backhanded Alice across the face, sending her stumbling backwards, and she fell flat into the river in front of Hook and Wendy, which sent an almighty wave of water over the pair of them and drenched Victor, Van Helsing, and Elizabeth, who joined them on the bridge.

'Stay back,' Wendy said, turning to her friends for a moment. 'She's mine.'

Wendy blocked attack after attack and eventually felt in control of the fight. She also felt something she hadn't expected. Fun. She was having fun and wasn't sure how to feel about that.

Hook managed to knock Wendy back a few steps and the two women locked eyes. Hook smiled, and then Wendy did something that she wasn't expecting.

She smiled back.

Hook's smile dropped from her face, and Wendy darted forward and took Hook by surprise with an array of attacks, all with a beaming smile on her face.

Cthulhu spread his giant wings and flapped them hard. Slowly, he took off from the ground and headed into the sky.

Alice reached out from the river and took a firm

hold of his left ankle and brought him back down to Earth. She threw him onto the land and delivered blow after blow to his slimy head.

Hook couldn't keep up with Wendy's attacks and rapidly backed up until she stood right in front of the portal device. With three quick strikes, Wendy disarmed Hook, sent her sword into the river, and cut her legs so that she fell to her knees.

Victorious, Wendy pointed her sword at Hook's throat.

Hook clasped her hands together. 'Please, Wendy ... show mercy.'

Wendy winked and brought her glowing green blade through Hook's wrists, sending both hands, still clasped together, flying into the river.

Hook let out a blood-curdling scream and held her scorched wrists up to her face. Wendy brought the blade back and with a single swipe, lopped off her head, which fell to the ground and came to a rest next to Wendy's feet.

Victor ran up to the portal device and tampered with the settings. 'I think I can open a portal to Ninety-Three Million Miles below us.'

'What exactly is Ninety-Three Million Miles below us?' Elizabeth asked.

'The sun.' Victor aimed the device directly onto the river. 'One big hole on the surface of the river should do it if Alice can get him in.'

Victor activated the portal device while Cthulhu and Alice continued to wrestle on the north bank of the river, but nothing happened.

'No power,' Victor said. 'It's not connected to my batteries, and I can't power the damn thing.'

Cthulhu grabbed hold of Alice's neck and threw her into the ground. Sparks flew out of the electrodes, which surrounded her overalls, and all of a sudden she shrank.

'Oh no,' Van Helsing said. 'He's broken her suit.'

Cthulhu lifted Alice into the air, and she became lighter and lighter as she decreased in size. He threw her into the river, and she landed next to what was left of Westminster Bridge, spluttering and trying to keep afloat as her suit failed and shocked her over and over again.

Van Helsing ran to the edge of the bridge. 'Alice! Are you all right?'

Alice had difficulty staying afloat, and Victor joined Van Helsing, looking down at her.

'Alice,' Victor said. 'You don't need the suit to use your powers. Those electrodes are completely useless. They're just a placebo, created to give you a feeling of control, but the power has always come from you.'

Van Helsing looked astonished at Victor's revelation. Alice disappeared under the water. Van Helsing kicked off her boots and dove into the water after her.

'Should I help?' Elizabeth asked.

Victor shook his head. 'No, we need to get the portal device working.' Together, they ran back to his machine.

Cthulhu made his way toward them. Though they may be insects to him, they had become a nuisance and had garnered his attention.

Victor tried hooking up Elizabeth's power supply to the machine, but it wasn't enough. There didn't seem to be any way of turning on his contraption.

'Frankenstein,' a small but powerful voice behind them yelled. Tinker Bell and Roxton made their way toward Victor, propping each other up while they left a bloody trail behind them. 'Get the device ready,' Tink said. 'I'll power it up.'

Cthulhu stepped closer. Tink grabbed hold of the device, and with a short burst of green energy, powered the machine up. Victor aimed it at the water in front of Cthulhu and turned it on.

Cthulhu brought his foot down hard onto the nub of bridge left over from his rampage and sent the portal device flying across the ground as it activated its intense beam of energy upwards into the sky.

The portal opened up two thousand feet above them with the blue grid inside flashing with pink lightning.

Victor yelled out in frustration. He sat up and watched Cthulhu prepare to finish them all off with another stomp of his foot.

Van Helsing surfaced below them, took a deep breath of air, and swam for the bank. 'Everyone get back.' A pair of naked, fleshy giant shoulders broke the surface of the water, followed by a giant head and giant arms.

Alice lifted her naked body out of the river and stood up, towering over Cthulhu, and then she grabbed him by his neck. She looked up at the portal above her and kept growing.

Cthulhu kicked and punched at her body, but the fury in Alice wouldn't allow her to feel any pain. She kept getting larger and larger. When she altered her footing, she stepped back onto Big Ben and knocked it over.

Alice stood two thousand feet tall and held Cthulhu up in one hand while he continued to roar and scream at her. She brought him close to her face and snapped her jaws around his head, pulling it off with her teeth.

She looked up at the portal above her, spat out his tentacle covered face into the glowing grid, and threw the rest of his body into it too.

The portal closed, and Alice breathed out a sigh and closed her eyes.

The others watched as she shrank down to normal size and passed out next to the Houses of Parliament.

'I don't believe it,' Roxton said. He crouched down, holding his leg tightly, picked up a cigarette from the ground, and placed it in his mouth. 'I don't suppose anyone has a light, do they?'

CHAPTER TWENTY-ONE

NEVER GO OUT WITH A WHIMPER

While Elizabeth stood at the foot of their bed, Victor took in her immense beauty. He had created her body, but her mind remained a purely unique thing; something he could never duplicate, and something he had missed so much that not even death could keep him from getting it back.

The extra-dimensional pirate invasion and ancient giant god rampage had been mere inconveniences; In the way of the two of them being together, and now it was over.

The authorities had arrested every last pirate, with all of them making the country's prisons a little more overcrowded. Mycroft had asked Victor to use his machine to send them all back to Neverland, but he'd refused. He told him his portal device had been destroyed in the fight with Cthulhu. A slight lie, perhaps —the machine could always be repaired in a few months —but Victor had given his word to Tink, as she lay on the surgical table of Victor's lab, that he wouldn't put Neverland in danger. The ambulance crew had patched up Roxton without much hassle, but Tinker Bell had a uniquely different physiology, and they were uncertain of her fate.

Victor had left Tink with Wendy and the others so that they could tend to her wounds. It may have been selfish, but Victor had taken these last few minutes for himself and Elizabeth, and holding her in his arms once more had given the rocky past few years of his life meaning.

He looked deeply into her vivacious eyes. 'I love you, Elizabeth Frankenstein,' he said. 'My heart will always belong to you.'

'But my heart ...' she said, looking back at him with a solemn, sober stare. 'Belongs to someone else.'

Alice thumped on their bedroom door. 'Doctor Frankenstein, come quickly, it's Tinker Bell.'

Victor and Elizabeth ran into the lab, where the rest of their team surrounded Tink, who lay on the table, looking pale and deathly ill.

'You have to do something,' Wendy said. 'You can't let them both die.'

Victor walked forward and put his hand on Tink's forehead. 'How do you help a being of such magic?'

'You can't,' Tink said with a breathless, strained voice. 'It's my time.'

Elizabeth placed her hand on Victor's arm, and he turned to look at her face. She glowed with goodness, kindness, and such relentless caring. Just as she had before she died. Victor hurt from the very core of his body. He could see that this truly was his wife returned to him, but he had achieved it through deception and pain. Elizabeth knew she'd never feel quite right in her body, and now Victor knew it too. A single tear fell down his cheek. 'There is something I can do.'

Elizabeth lay on the surgical table in the middle of the lab, next to the body of Peter. Victor opened the young man's green leather vest and prepped his chest for surgery while Wendy stood next to him.

They'd made Tinker Bell comfortable on her table, with a pillow under her head and a warm blanket over her body. She watched as Victor prepared to sacrifice everything he had worked for in order to bring back her friend.

Wendy walked over to Tink and held her hand. 'Can I ask you something?' she said.

'Of course,' Tink said quietly.

'How come you never came to see Peter?'

'Is that what he thought?' she said. 'That I never came looking for him?'

'You did, then?'

'Let me ask you, if your life partner ran away to be with someone else and you one day decided to look them up, but as you reached their window... in their new house... in their new life, you saw them happier than they ever were with you... would you knock on that window?'

You didn't need adventures and magic anymore. You just needed each other. Who am I to spoil that?'

Wendy burst into tears and hugged Tink.

'Okay ... not so hard,' Tink said. 'I'm dying here.'

Victor walked over to his wife, and she took his hand, giving him a reassuring smile.

Wendy wiped the tears from her eyes and looked over at Victor. 'What if it doesn't work?'

'It'll work,' Victor said. He seemed unsure. He turned back to Elizabeth and kissed her lips. 'Elizabeth, I'm sorry.'

'Don't be sorry.' Elizabeth's eyes teared up in beautiful contrast to her heart-warming smile. 'You gave me an amazing gift. I got to see you one last time, and for that I will always be grateful. But this is the right thing to do.'

She was right. Throughout their relationship, she always had been. He wished he had listened to her more. For all his genius, Victor was never as smart as Elizabeth. She knew the difference between right and wrong, which seemed to be a struggle for a great many people in the world.

Victor pressed his head against hers. 'Goodbye, my love.'

'Goodbye, Victor,' Elizabeth said. 'You have been my world. Now go live your life.'

She smiled, and Victor's tears dropped onto her chest as he placed the plastic mask over her face. She closed her eyes and took a long deep breath, which would be her last.

At 4:15 a.m., Roxton walked into the lab looking concerned. Victor had just finished sewing Peter's chest back up; he felt exhausted, tired, and emotionally drained.

Roxton pointed to the window. 'There's no lightning out there.' Though the storm from earlier had long passed, the night remained dark and cloudy. 'How are you going to power this machine of yours, Frankenstein?'

Victor didn't have an answer for him. Peter had gone unpreserved for too long. As he hooked up the electrodes to Peter's body, Victor questioned whether his reanimation technique would even work. Eventually, he said, 'That is in the hands of fate.'

'Screw that, Doctor,' Tink said. She then pulled off

her blanket, got to her feet, and held her bandaged stomach. 'I'll get you the energy you need.'

Tinker Bell staggered toward the door, and Wendy grabbed hold of her.

'Tink ... what are you doing?'

Tink turned to her and smiled. 'I never did want to go out with a whimper.' In a burst of fairy dust, she shrank to her natural fairy form and flew out of the door at speed.

Victor raced over to his equipment, took out a syringe of his regenerative solution, and plunged it into Peter's heart.

———

Tinker Bell flew out of the front door of Frankenstein Manor and headed up into the sky, directly above the house. She held her stomach tightly as her green plasma wings fluttered away behind her, taking her further up through the moist clouds.

The energy contained within her body had been leaking out of her, but since her friends had bandaged and plugged her wounds, the energy had built up. Her tiny form was like a fusion reactor; so much power stored in such a small being. But her core had been ruptured, and she was about to go nuclear.

Tink came to a halt among the clouds, closed her eyes, and strained her body until every atom inside her shook at a relentless speed. The very fibre of her being could no longer hold together.

She let go of her stomach, whipped her arms out by her side, threw her head back with an almighty scream, and exploded with incandescent green light, spreading out along the sky, and filling the clouds with such unbelievable energy.

A bright green lightning bolt shot out of the thundering sky and struck the antenna on Frankenstein's roof, tearing the very slates off, and setting the entire right-hand side of the house on fire.

Victor's lab powered up with an intense bright light and his equipment burst into life, with a whirring electrical noise that nearly deafened both Victor and Wendy.

Victor pulled the focusing device, so it pointed directly at Peter's body, and then headed to the lever on the wall near his equipment and grabbed hold of it. He caught Wendy's eye... and smiled.

Victor pulled the lever, sending waves of incredible green electricity through Peter's body. The glass in Victor's equipment exploded along with the light bulbs and his huge batteries.

Wendy fell to the ground when a barrage of green sparks flew across the lab, setting the place on fire.

Peter's body writhed and tensed, and half the ceiling fell around them and onto Victor's table of machinery, cutting the power.

Peter's body lunged forward and sat up, letting out an intense and painful cry, and all at once, everything went quiet and dark and still.

Pockets of fire, coming from the equipment around them, provided the sole remaining light in the room. Wendy got to her feet and ran over to Peter, screaming his name, hoping he wouldn't backhand her into the wall, as Elizabeth had done to Victor. She touched his shoulder. It felt warm. Hot, even. 'Peter?' she said.

Peter turned his head and looked at Wendy. The dawn sun crept in through the laboratory window, hitting the back of Peter's head and lighting up Wendy's face. He looked into her eyes and smiled. 'I feel... happy!'

———

Peter and Wendy stood in the stony driveway of Frankenstein manor while the hot sun beamed down upon them. They looked out into the sky, and then turned back to see Victor walk out to join them, along with Van Helsing, Alice, and Roxton.

Wendy ran up to Victor and hugged him tightly. 'Thank you,' she said.

'Where are you headed?' he asked.

Peter looked out at the blue sky. 'Second to the right... straight on 'til morning.'

Peter took Wendy's hand. They raced off down the driveway and took off, flying into the air, hand in hand.

The beaming faces of their friends watched as they disappeared through the clouds, but quickly became distracted when a black limousine pulled up on the driveway.

Mycroft Holmes stepped out and walked up to Victor, returning their concerned looks with a bemused smile. 'Jail-breaking, assault of police officers, obstruction of justice, unlicensed experimentation, endangering the public—I could go on.'

'I think we get the idea,' Victor said. 'Are we in trouble?'

'That depends.' Mycroft lit a cigarette and offered another to Roxton, who accepted gladly.

'Depends on what, exactly?' Victor asked.

'On whether you're willing to do some work for us? The Germans are making some trouble overseas. I think this League of yours could be a rather handy asset.'

'We're not soldiers, Mr Holmes,' Van Helsing said.

'What kind of pay packet are we looking at here?' Roxton asked.

'Oh, I'm sure we can work out something to suit you.' Mycroft took in a deep breath of smoke and exhaled into the air.

While Peter and Wendy rose above the clouds, the wind blew over their faces. They flew up through the atmosphere and out into space, feeling the warm sun hit their bodies.

They continued heading towards a speck in the distance until their two bodies were so far away from Earth that both of them and the tiny glowing speck seemed like one.

THE END